Octavia Boone's
Big Questions
About Life,
the Universe,
and Everything

OCTAVIA BOONE'S
BIG
QUESTIONS
ABOUT LIFE,
THE
UNIVERSE,
..AND..
EVERYTHING

Rebecca Rupp

CANDLEWICK PRESS

First edition 2010

Library of Congress Cataloging-in-Publication Data

Rupp, Rebecca.
Octavia Boone's big questions about life, the universe, and everything /
Rebecca Rupp. — 1st U.S. ed.
p. cm.
Summary: Seventh-grader Octavia puzzles over life's biggest questions when
her mother seems to find the answers in a conservative Christian church, while
her artist father believes the writings of Henry David Thoreau hold the key.
ISBN 978-0-7636-4491-8
[1. Religions — Fiction. 2. Family life — Vermont — Fiction.
3. Schools — Fiction. 4. Christian life — Fiction. 5. Vermont — Fiction.]
I. Title.
PZ7.R8886Oct 2010
[Fic] — dc22   2009047408

10 11 12 13 14 15 RRC 10 9 8 7 6 5 4 3 2 1

Printed in Crawfordsville, IN, U.S.A.

This book was typeset in Adobe Caslon.

Candlewick Press
99 Dover Street
Somerville, Massachusetts 02144

visit us at www.candlewick.com

For free thinkers everywhere

CHAPTER I

MR. JEREMIAH PEACOCK, our neighbor, can always tell when a thunderstorm is coming. This is because of his Ominous Knee. When his knee twinges, that means a thunderstorm is on the way.

The Ominous Knee once saved his life, says Mr. Peacock, because it was twinging on the day Mrs. Peacock wanted him to put up an aluminum umbrella clothesline in the backyard, and if he'd done what she wanted, Mr. Peacock says, he would have been out there waving a big old aluminum pole around when the storm rolled in and the lightning would have killed him deader than hell.

"What's twinging like?" I said.

I thought it was a cool word, *twinging*. Kind of copper-colored, like those expensive French frying pans.

Mr. Peacock fixed me with his good right eye and said I should thank my lucky stars I didn't know, since it was like red-hot needles straight from Old Nick's furnace, which, even so, didn't cause half the pain and suffering he'd had for the past fifty-three years putting up with Mrs. Peacock's mims and twitters. Though I think he was just joking about the second part because Mrs. Peacock is very even-tempered, and besides, she weighs two hundred pounds and never twitters at all.

Since then, though, I've thought more than once that an Ominous Knee might be a good thing to have. At least it gives you some warning when something awful's coming so that trouble doesn't catch you unprepared.

Because looking back, I was pretty clueless. At the beginning of the year that changed my life, the only thing I was worrying about was my name.

* * *

According to *Seventeen* magazine, the most popular names for girls are Emily, Emma, Madison, Abigail, Isabella, Hannah, Samantha, Ava, Ashley, and Olivia.

This is mine: Octavia. Octavia O'Keeffe Boone.

My name is so far from a popular name that if you set me down next to somebody named Emily, the pair of us would probably just explode, like when matter meets antimatter.

The O'Keeffe is from Georgia O'Keeffe, who is famous for painting cow skulls and flowers the size of pizza platters. Boone, being a painter, thought I should have a strong female painter's name in mine. The Octavia was Ray's idea, probably while she was coming out of anesthesia.

What I don't understand is why Boone and Ray couldn't see that giving me a stupid name like that made my initials O.O.B., OOB, which is just one letter away from BOOB. But then Boone was always so busy painting his masterpiece that he never noticed anything, and Ray has always been a person who makes decisions first and thinks about them afterward. In other words, when it came to naming babies, they were a perfect lethal storm.

I'll bet that by the time I was two days old, Ray was realizing her mistake and wishing she'd named me Ashley or Abigail. Not that she'll ever say so, because another thing about Ray is that she will never admit she's wrong. Once when I complained, she just said I should be glad she hadn't named me Cantaloupe or Pomegranate, like all those celebrities who keep naming their kids after fruit, or maybe just @, like this Chinese baby she read about on the Internet.

Ray's real name is Rachel.

Boone's real name is Simon, but nobody calls him that except Ray.

"How come everybody calls you Boone?" I asked him once, and first he said it was because all great painters went by their last names, and you didn't hear anybody going around calling Picasso Pablo, did you?

But then he said actually it was because of this cross-eyed kid named Woody Schaffer who kept calling him Simple Simon in third grade.

You'd think that with that in his background, Boone at least would have been more sensitive about names.

I guess there's still a part of me that thinks maybe none of this would have happened if Boone and Ray had been the sort of parents to give a kid a normal name, like Jane or Susan or Mary Ann. I think about the kinds of lives Janes and Susans probably have, where their fathers go to an office and their mothers bake stuff and run the PTO. I bet Janes and Susans just have normal problems, like whether they can go to the mall on a school night or get their noses pierced or wear shorts to school.

To be fair, most kids around here don't have popular names either, but at least they have strength in numbers since they're all unpopular in the same way. Most of them have French names like Claude and Cecile and Armand and Solange, because our town is in a part of Vermont that is just eleven miles from the French part of Canada, which is where Boone always says he's going to move to every time he hears something he doesn't like on NPR.

On the other hand, I am not alone in hating my name. Angelique Soulier says that no matter what her mother says and no matter how many times her French great-grandmother rolls over in the grave, the minute she turns eighteen, she's changing her name to Jennifer.

My best friend, Andrew Wochak, does not hate his name, but unfortunately nobody calls Andrew Andrew, except me, his parents, and the teachers at school. Everybody else calls him Woodchuck. This is because Wochak sounds sort of like Woodchuck, and also because Andrew has furry brown hair and his front teeth stick out, though that is being corrected by braces.

The reason I do not call Andrew Woodchuck is because of an invisible penguin.

When I was very young, I had a secret friend named Priscilla who was a penguin. Nobody could see Priscilla but me. She went everywhere with me and she slept at the foot of my bed and I saved food for her off my plate, especially stuff like Brussels sprouts and oatmeal. Ray told me once that she worried because I had made Priscilla so real that Ray was always doing things like opening the door for Priscilla or leaving the window rolled down a little if Priscilla had to wait for us in the car.

Then Priscilla went with me to kindergarten.

Sixty-five percent of children under the age of seven at some point have an imaginary friend. I read that somewhere. What that means is that out of every ten little kids you see, six and a half of them have an invisible pal hanging around.

But you wouldn't have thought so to hear Mrs. Baines, the kindergarten teacher, when I asked for extra purple finger paint for Priscilla.

"For *whom*?" she said, and she looked at me down her pug nose, that made her look like one of those sniffy flat-faced little Pekingese dogs.

Then she called us all together for Attention Time, which meant that we had to be quiet and listen whenever she held up her thumb, and gave us a long lecture about being big kids now, old enough to go to school and much too old for silly things like imaginary invisible penguins. Everybody stared at me and a couple of kids in the back giggled and my face got hot and I wanted the floor to open up under me and swallow me along with my little strawberry-colored plastic chair.

Then Mrs. Baines said in that smarmy voice some kindergarten teachers use, "Now you all know that things that are invisible aren't real, don't you, children? They're just make-believe."

And then Andrew Wochak raised his hand and said, "Well, what about air?"

I will never as long as I live call Andrew Woodchuck.

Mrs. Baines doesn't teach kindergarten anymore. The School Board fired her.

Here is my word for Andrew: *Outstanding*.

CHAPTER 2

I LIKE *O* WORDS like *Outstanding* because my brain is cross-wired.

I am a synesthetic.

Synesthetics have their senses somehow crossed up and mixed together, so that they can hear colors or taste shapes. To some synesthetics, chocolate tastes like cylinders and pickles taste like triangles, and to others red makes a high whiny sound and harp music is dark gold. I read that people can have synesthetic experiences on psychedelic drugs like LSD, but Boone told me not to even think of going there. Boone had a checkered college career and he should know.

My kind of synesthesia is called grapheme, which means that I see letters as having colors and textures. Sometimes I see words that way too. It's kind of cool, really, though Mrs. Baines didn't like it any more than she liked Priscilla. To me, *M* is fuzzy and pink and *T* is black and thorny, like barbed wire. *A* is dark green and *Q* is like old waxed wood and *O* is cool and smooth and polished and pale, like a silver bracelet. *O* is my favorite letter. I love *O*s.

For my birthday the year I turned eleven, Ray and Boone gave me *The Wonderful O* by James Thurber, which is still my favorite book of all time. It's about a pirate named Black who hates the letter *O* because his mother once got wedged in a porthole and, since they couldn't pull her in, they ended up pushing her out, and that was the end of her.

Then Black and his pirate crew, while out searching for treasure, ended up taking over an island where they abolished everything with the letter *O* in it: clocks and shoes and spoons and poodles and oboes. Bakers lost their dough and goldsmiths lost their gold and tailors lost their cloth. *School* became *schl* and the *moon* became *mn*. Soon everyone discovered how awful the world would be without the letter *O*. Because life's most important words are words with *O*s in them.

Like *love* and *hope* and *freedom* and *tomorrow*.

You would think that an *O* person like me would live in Ohio or Oklahoma, or maybe Colorado, but I don't, because way back before I was born, when Ray and Boone were picking a place to live, they weren't thinking about *O*s but about clean air and natural fibers and making their own granola. Which is why we live in Winton Falls, Vermont, though as Boone points out, it could have been worse, because they also considered Maine, New Hampshire, and Massachusetts, which have no *O*s in them at all.

So during most of the year that changed my life, I was in the seventh grade at the Winton Falls Elementary and Middle School K–8. We are a combined school because Winton Falls is a really small town and there aren't enough of us for two schools. Kids from Winton Falls can't go to high school here, because there isn't one, but have to take the bus into Wolverton, which is fifteen miles away.

Even though it's a small school with a budget that Mr. Peacock says isn't big enough to spit at, we still do a lot of stuff. We have sports teams, a drama club, and a Maple Sugar Festival, that Ray always said was a dastardly plot between the town dentist and the pharmaceutical companies that sell anti-hyperactivity pills, and we have an annual science fair.

The science fair is a really big deal and it was a big part of the year that changed my life, though it certainly didn't work out the way I'd planned. It's held every spring in the cafeteria, and every year Andrew Wochak fails to win it, not because he is not brilliant but because he is subject to serious miscalculations. Last year, in sixth grade, for example, he built a cabbage catapult, which would have won, except that his demonstration cabbage broke the windshield of Mr. Clover Harrison's Dodge pickup, and Mr. Clover Harrison is on the School Board.

After that the judges outlawed any projects that involved the hurling of missiles.

By the first day of school, Andrew always had a plan ready for his science fair project, but he would never tell me what it was because, he said, he didn't want to ruin the surprise. That basically meant that he was planning something so potentially horrible that he didn't want any word of it getting out ahead of time. I should mention here that the Wochaks as a family are known to be prone to disaster.

This is the sort of thing you know living in a small town, where everybody knows everything about everybody else. For example, like how the Dufresnes, given a choice, always turn the wrong way at an intersection, and the Thibodeaus are what Mrs. Peacock calls poison-neat and never take the protective plastic covers off their living-room chairs, and the Harrisons are tight with money and mean as two-headed snakes. Though in Mr. Clover Harrison's case this last could be because of growing up with a name like Clover, which must have been very warping for a boy.

Anyway, what with Andrew being a Wochak, his surprises are not something to look forward to. Actually no surprises are, in my opinion, because in my experience surprises usually turn out to be bad. Like when Mr. and Mrs. Jeremiah Peacock had their fiftieth wedding anniversary, their daughter Sandy, who lives in Ohio, gave them a surprise party. The surprise caught Mr. Peacock asleep in the TV room in his polka-dot boxer shorts and Mrs. Peacock with pink plastic curlers in her hair, and Sandy said afterward that living in Ohio was not nearly far enough away.

Not liking surprises is also the reason that I always read the ends of books first. Ray says this is a terrible habit, and if authors knew I did this, they would track me to the ends of the earth and take away my library card. But I like to know where things are going. I like to know who's going to live and who's going to die, and in mysteries, I like to know who the criminal is right from the beginning. I've always wished real life could be like that, that you could peek ahead every once in a while, just to see what's going to happen.

The first day of school that fall, Ms. Hodges, the seventh-grade teacher, had us discuss our plans for the future. Ms. Hodges has frizzy black hair and she wears sneakers and cardigan sweaters with pockets that always made me think of Mr. Rogers on old shows on TV. It's important to think ahead, Ms. Hodges said, because then you have a better chance of getting where you want to go. She was always urging us to establish goals and set benchmarks and keep our eyes on the ball. That first day she made us all take turns telling where we planned to be in ten years.

Jean-Claude Chevalier, who wears a leather jacket and shaves his head bald, said he was going to be a policeman like his uncle Joe, though without the belly and the high blood pressure. He also planned to have a yacht and a motorcycle and a whole bunch of girlfriends who look like Pamela Anderson.

Polly Pelletier, whose mother runs the Creative Clip Shoppe on Main Street, said she was going to be a fashion designer. Her line of clothes will be called Polli, with an *i*. Polly is really into clothes. Her favorite TV show is *Project Runway,* and her favorite movie is *The Devil Wears Prada,* except that she doesn't think the devil does.

Aaron Pennebaker, who is nearsighted and short for his age, said he was going to make movies about large and powerful superheroes. It is not Aaron's fault that he is short, though I think his parents should have considered human growth hormone injections instead of relying solely on whole milk and vitamin pills. All the Pennebaker men tend to be on the short side, which, as I said, is the sort of thing you know living in a small town.

Celeste Olavson, who is the captain of the hockey team, is going to be a physical therapist, which seems only fair what with the number of people she's practically crippled by whacking them with her hockey stick. Celeste is half Scandinavian and the descendant of murderous Viking marauders.

Angelique Soulier is going to be a small-animal veterinarian and have four children, two boys and two girls, but she isn't going to give up her job to stay home with them because she thinks it's important for women to be strong role models. Of course by this time she will have changed her name to Jennifer.

When it was my turn, I still hadn't made up my mind what I was going to say. That kind of discussion always makes me want to say something weird just to be different, like I want to be a blacksmith or a circus performer or a sculptor who makes things out of cheese. Boone says that's because I have contrary genes.

But Ms. Hodges was giving us her hard look, which meant that she didn't want to hear any more smart answers about yachts and Pamela Anderson, so what I said was that I'd like to be a scientist. Because I think that if people applied the scientific method to their lives, there would be fewer problems in the world.

When I said that later to Ray, she said, "Oh, *please*, Octavia," which has always been Ray's way of saying "You are so full of crap." For a lawyer, Ray has always been surprisingly illogical.

Ray was still a lawyer then. She was a partner at a firm in Burlington called Banger & Moss, which specializes in environmental law. They prosecute people who dump stuff in the rivers and keep developers from building shopping malls on top of bird sanctuaries and beaver dams. Boone always called Ray's law firm Bangers & Mash, which is a joke about sausages. Bangers and mash is sausage and potatoes. You get it to eat at British pubs. Boone is a master of feeble jokes.

Ray was never a vicious lawyer like they show in those cartoons about sharks with briefcases. Ray believes in the importance of feelings. She always says that the heart knows more than the brain. Also, being an environmental lawyer, she was suspicious of science because of the atom bomb and genetically engineered crops and chemical pollution.

Here is where Ray was wrong: the heart doesn't know more than the brain. In fact, the heart doesn't know anything at all because it's just a big lump of muscle.

Also, feelings aren't reliable.

In sixth grade, Polly Pelletier and Sara Boudreau were such good friends that they always dressed alike and wore the same color nail polish and stayed overnight at each other's houses all the time and even got little matching rosebud tattoos. By the beginning of seventh grade, due to an irrevocable emotional occurrence over the summer, they weren't even speaking to each other.

Also last spring, Andrew, who should have known better, fell madly in love with Julie Laroche. For eight entire weeks, he was a blue-whale-size pain. He hung around Julie all the time looking moon-eyed, and whenever I saw him, all he wanted to talk about was whether or not she'd said anything about him and whether or not she liked him. This was difficult for me since I happened to know that Julie was in love with Jean-Claude Chevalier. She has a thing for bald men potentially about to be in uniform.

But clueless Andrew couldn't see it. He even wrote her a poem, which I can predict is going to come back someday to haunt him, like those naked pictures your parents take of you when you're a baby in the bathtub.

Feelings make you do stupid stuff. Feelings get you into trouble.

With feelings you never know where you are.

CHAPTER 3

WHERE IT REALLY ALL STARTED was with Ray.

Ray, for as long as I'd known her, and which, since she's my mother, has been my entire life, had been a seeker. She was a seeker long before me too, but nothing she'd found had ever worked out very well.

First she was seeking for world peace and universal justice, and she went to rallies, and Boone has a picture of her with about a million other people marching on the mall in Washington, D.C. But nothing ever came of that because of big business and the oil companies and the military-industrial complex actually running the country.

Then she was seeking for women's rights and sisterhood, and she belonged to a lot of consciousness-raising groups and stopped shaving her legs and washing her hair. But that didn't work out either because, even though Ray believes in equal pay for equal work, she got sick of belonging to book clubs that wouldn't read books if the authors were males.

After that she was an environmental activist, and she belonged to this guerrilla gardeners' society that used to sneak into parks and vacant lots and plant tomatoes when no one was looking. That was when she decided to go to law school and study environmental law. She was still seeking to save the planet then, but she figured it wouldn't hurt to save it while earning a regular salary, with health benefits.

That was when she met Boone, who was working as a financial planner and painting on the side, which was stifling his creative flow. So after Ray graduated from law school, they moved to Vermont, because by then Ray was seeking the simple life and Boone was willing to do anything that would let him paint in the daytime. They were planning to live on a farm and raise organic vegetables and free-range chickens and make their own maple syrup and toothpaste and yogurt, and Ray was going to learn to weave. But that didn't work out either because first they had cutworms, and then Ray turned out to be allergic to chicken feathers, and when they boiled the sap to make maple syrup, all the wallpaper in the kitchen peeled off. So they gave up and moved into town, which is when they had me.

Actually Boone never totally gave up on the simple life, because he still had a garden in the yard beside his painting shed. Also he was always quoting Henry David Thoreau, who was famous for living at Walden Pond in a house he built by himself, growing his own beans, and then writing a book about it.

Boone would say things like "'Do not lose hold of your dreams or aspirations. For if you do, you may still exist but you have ceased to live.'" Once when Ray bought a new living-room couch, he said, "'I would rather sit on a pumpkin and have it all to myself than be crowded on a velvet cushion.'"

Ray said that he could sit on a pumpkin all he wanted, but she was sick of the broken springs poking her in the behind.

Anyway the new couch was not velvet. It was blue plaid.

But Ray never stopped seeking, and ever since I was eight or nine or so, she'd been seeking for spiritual fulfillment and the deeper meaning of life. Basically that meant that she kept trying all these different churches, but none of the ones she tried was ever right because she never liked any of them enough to settle down.

For Winton Falls this was weird, since people here don't change much when it comes to religion. Most of the French kids are Catholic, like their parents and grandparents and great-grandparents probably all the way back to Saint Peter, and they go to the Church of the Holy Nativity at the end of Spring Street. The Protestant kids are mostly Methodists, Baptists, Congregationalists, or Episcopalians. Aaron Pennebaker and Jeannie Greenberg are Jewish, and Earl Barney is a Jehovah's Witness and goes to the Kingdom Hall over on Route 7A. But whatever people are here, they usually stay that way.

Except Ray. She kept switching from place to place all the time, trying to find her perfect spiritual fit. She made me think of a book I had when I was little called *The Missing Piece,* which was about this sad little circle with a triangle-shaped chunk taken out of it, rolling around the world searching for the perfect little triangle that would make it whole. She took classes in yoga breathing and she tried the Way of Tao Meditation Center in Richford, and for a while she went to Wiccan meetings with a woman named Clarice who wore caftans and necklaces shaped like pentagrams. For a couple of months she even belonged to the Enlightened Brethren, who met every week in somebody's garage and talked about the end of the world. And she tried all the regular churches too.

Boone used to say that Ray shopped for spiritual experiences the way other women shopped for shoes, and he'd joke about the flavor of the month. Boone wasn't seeking. He was happy with oil paint and Henry David Thoreau.

The first hint I had that Ray had found something new came on a Sunday morning at the beginning of August before school had started. I could tell by the way Ray came up the stairs, fast, with her heels clicking on the steps like castanets. She only did that if something big was up and we were late for it. She poked her head in the doorway of my bedroom, where I was lying on my bed reading *Anne of Green Gables*. I had just reached the part where Anne had bought hair dye from a peddler and it turned her hair green.

"Octavia, you're not dressed yet," Ray said.

Second hint.

"Yes, I am," I said, because I was. I was wearing jeans and a T-shirt.

"I must have forgotten to tell you," Ray said, which made me suspicious right there. Ray never forgot anything.

"Tell me what?" I said.

"We're going to a new church," Ray said. She sounded bright, but a little nervy, the way people do when they're talking up something that they know in their heart of hearts you're going to hate. By this time, I'd been to enough new churches (etc.) with Ray to last a lifetime.

"I don't want to go," I said. "I want to stay home with Boone."

Boone does not go to church. He says that spiritual experiences are not meant to be social events. Ray says that Boone is a hopeless cause.

After all the dragging around to churches, I wished Ray would consider me a hopeless cause too, but when I asked, she wouldn't go for it. To be a hopeless cause, Ray said, you have to be over twenty-five.

"I want you to give this a chance," Ray said. "I've been there several times, and they're lovely people. You might actually enjoy yourself. Get up out of there and put on that nice green skirt. And comb your hair."

"I'm reading," I said.

"You can read when we get home," Ray said.

Looking back, it was right then that I wish I'd had an Ominous Knee.

Because then I'd have had some warning. It would have been twinging all over the place, telling me of the coming storm.

CHAPTER 4

RAY'S LATEST WAS CALLED the Fellowship of the Redeemer, and it was in Wolverton, where the high school is, because by then Ray had pretty much exhausted everything in Winton Falls. The Redeemers met in what used to be the Cadillac Motel. Ray pulled into the motel parking lot, which was practically full. On either side of us there were bumper stickers that read RIGHT TO LIFE, HONK IF YOU LOVE JESUS, and DUCKS UNLIMITED. Where the motel sign used to be it now said FELLOWSHIP HALL OF THE REDEEMER in big black letters. The Redeemers had kept the old motel VACANCY sign though, which still dangled beneath the bigger sign on little chains.

"What's that all about?" I said. "Are they still renting rooms?"

Ray gave me a look.

"It's a friendly gesture to show that there's always room for new members," she said. "I think it's funny. I told you, Octavia, these people are nice."

But then she'd said that about the Enlightened Brethren too, who in my opinion were about as nice as a coven of ax murderers.

Inside, what used to be the motel lobby was now decorated with potted palms, red drapes with gold cords, crosses, and a lot of framed photographs of famous Redeemers, including one of a lady with her hands folded and her eyes turned up soulfully as if she was trying to see her own eyebrows. What used to be the motel bedrooms were now all meeting rooms and classrooms, which I thought was pretty funny considering the reputation of the Cadillac Motel, and there were now tables and chairs and black-boards where the beds and the TVs for the X-rated movies used to be.

Ray took me to Room 12 (No Smoking), which was where I was going to be educated while she was off in the ex-motel conference center being spiritually fulfilled. Inside there were about a dozen kids sitting around a table, and they all stared at me when I walked in the door. The teacher was all over Ray. You'd have thought they were long-lost sisters.

"Rachel!" she said. She had one of those voices that reminded me somehow of chocolate. "I meant to call to tell you how much I enjoyed our talk last week. And I'm so glad that you've brought your daughter. She's a beauty, Rachel."

Which was laying it on super-thick because I am no beauty. I have straight brown hair and I am skinny and tall. Aaron Pennebaker calls me the Giraffe.

"This is Octavia, Janet," Ray said. "Octavia, this is Mrs. Prescott."

"She has your eyes," Mrs. Prescott said. And then to me, "Did you know, dear, that the eyes are windows to the soul?"

So this woman did not know anatomy.

Ray poked me in the back.

"Actually most people think I look like my father," I said.

Mrs. Prescott had round glasses with black plastic frames, bright brown eyes, streaky brown hair, and round pink cheeks. She reminded me of a cartoon I used to watch when I was a little kid about Chibby the Cheerful Chipmunk.

"I know you'll be a wonderful addition to our group, Octavia," Mrs. Prescott said, all chocolate and cheerful. She pointed to an empty folding chair. "Why don't you take a seat right over there, next to Marjean?"

I sat down, which I didn't want to do, and Ray and Mrs. Prescott hugged each other, and Ray, with barely a backward glance, took off, leaving me with a roomful of strangers. Also I had no escape route, since Ray had the car keys. Though of course even if I'd managed to nab them, I didn't know how to drive.

Marjean had freckles and a pair of thick blond braids that wrapped around her head. She was wearing a blue gingham pinafore dress with ruffles that looked like the sort of thing Laura Ingalls might have worn in *Little House on the Prairie.*

"You've got a really weird name," Marjean said.

I shrugged. I agreed with her totally, but I wasn't about to admit it.

"And your clothes are all wrong," Marjean said.

"What?" I said.

Thinking that Marjean was not exactly the person to give fashion advice. I wondered what Polly Pelletier would do if she ever got her hands on Marjean. Marjean was kind of cute actually, if you could get past the braids and the pinafore.

"When we fail to follow the rule of modesty, we create unwholesome thoughts in the minds of those who see us," Marjean said, sounding as if she was quoting somebody.

Based on my initial observations, it was clear that those who followed the rule of modesty were asking to be tortured laughingstocks in the seventh grade at Winton Falls Elementary and Middle School K–8.

I opened my mouth to say so, but just then Mrs. Prescott began clapping her hands and everybody had to shut up. It was clear to me that Marjean and I were not going to hit it off. Privately I decided to refer to Marjean from now on as Margarine.

"First," Mrs. Prescott said, "I'd like to introduce you all to our new class member, Octavia Boone. I know you'll all do your best to welcome Octavia and make her feel at home."

A kid at the foot of the table who was wearing a clip-on tie with a pattern of race cars on it nudged the kid next to him and said, "What was her name? Octopus?" and then laughed *haw-haw-haw* with his mouth open.

Mrs. Prescott said, "Octavia, we like to start our sessions each time by reminding us why we're all together here. We call this the Ceremony of Affirmation, and I hope that soon you'll feel ready to join in. I like to think that the Affirmation is like a golden chain, reminding us that no matter what our differences are, we're all bound together by love and faith."

She paused and peered brightly around the table.

"This time we'll start with you, Ronnie. Do you love Jesus and accept him as your personal savior?"

Ronnie was the *haw-haw* kid at the foot of the table. His ears, which were enormous, stuck out.

"Yes," Ronnie said.

I realized right then that I should never have gotten into the car with Ray. I should have wrapped my arms around the bedpost and screamed for Boone. I should have locked my door and shoved the bureau in front of it.

"Cathy Ann, do you love Jesus and accept him as your personal savior?"

Cathy Ann had curly dark hair pinned behind her ears with butterfly barrettes and a bandage on her chin. I wondered meanly if she'd done something awful with a pimple.

"Yes, I do," Cathy Ann said.

"Paul, do you love Jesus and accept him as your personal savior?"

Paul did. Then Ashley, Matthew, Marie, Marjean, Wesley, Todd, and Kristin all accepted Jesus as their personal saviors.

I decided that when we got home I was going to kill Ray.

I looked over Mrs. Prescott's head. Above her, hanging on the wall, was a color picture of Jesus. He had long wavy hair, rosy cheeks, and a dreamy expression. I wondered if he knew he was hanging in a room where for years and years people had been doing drug deals and committing adultery.

"Octavia, we all hope you'll be able to join with us next time," Mrs. Prescott said. "But we want you to know that we're all glad you're here. Let's all say a prayer of welcome for Octavia right now."

If there's anything more embarrassing than a roomful of people praying for you, I don't know what it is. And the hour that followed was possibly the longest of my life, and that's counting time in the dentist's chair getting a tooth drilled and in the emergency room at the hospital the day Andrew and I were pretending to be Tarzan and Cheetah on the swing and I broke my left arm. We had more prayers and then Bible readings and then a Bible verse quiz game, in which I came in last. Then Mrs. Prescott had everybody share stories about how God had helped them in their daily lives.

Ronnie said that last Saturday he lost the money his mother had given him to go to the movies, but he asked God for help and then he found a five-dollar bill under a bush.

Marjean told how she'd lost her math homework and couldn't find it anywhere, but she prayed and then she heard a voice in her head telling her where to look for it and she did and it was there.

What a waste of God's time, I thought. What if he was supposed to be off taking care of starving people in Africa but instead he has to turn around and help some whiny kids find stuff?

"Can you think of any times when God has helped you, Octavia?" Mrs. Prescott asked.

I decided to kill Ray with slow torture.

"No," I said.

Mrs. Prescott gave me a kindly smile.

"That's fine, Octavia," she said. "But I'm sure God has helped you many times, whether you realize it or not."

It seemed like a geological era before class was over and Ray came to collect me. When we left, Mrs. Prescott said she looked forward to seeing me next Sunday.

I thought that she could look forward until hell freezes over.

My *O* word for this experience: *Odious.*

CHAPTER 5

THE BIG QUESTIONS about life, the universe, and everything were Andrew's idea. He thought them up right at the beginning of the school year, in September, which is one of my favorite months even though it doesn't have an *O* in it, because September is such a beautiful blue-and-gold sort of word.

It was recess period at school. We were sitting on the grass at the edge of the playground after lunch, and Andrew was eating a cupcake. Andrew eats practically all the time. By all rights, he should be the size of one of those giant balloons in the Macy's Thanksgiving Day parade.

"My mother's hanging red ribbons in the car," Andrew said.

Andrew's parents are not weird in the same way as Boone and Ray, but they are weird all the same. Weird parents is one of the bonds Andrew and I have, along with our mutual hatred of Mrs. Baines, whose firing by the School Board we celebrated by toasting with ginger ale and then throwing firecrackers off Andrew's back porch until Andrew's mother caught us.

"How come?" I said.

"It's an auspicious color," Andrew said glumly. "It's supposed to adjust our energy and protect us from accidents."

Andrew's father is a Buddhist and his mother practices feng shui. Their house is full of crystals and wind chimes and bamboo plants, and there's a big mirror in the kitchen so that while cooking his mother will not experience negative *chi*. Andrew's bedroom is in their house's Wealth Corner, so he's not allowed to open the windows, even in summer, because of possibly causing wealth to flow out of the family savings account.

This has caused Andrew to decide to be a philosopher. Andrew thinks that the purpose of life is to search in a logical fashion for answers to the world's big questions, which he feels that his parents have not done.

"What makes you think life has a purpose?" I said.

"Because it has to," Andrew said. "We wouldn't be here on this planet just for nothing, would we?"

It seemed to me that a philosopher should have a better answer than that, but I didn't want to hurt Andrew's feelings.

It was a beautiful warm day, like a little piece of summer suddenly plopped down at the beginning of fall. Kids were running around without their jackets. Boone says this kind of weather is called Indian summer, but I'll bet it isn't anymore because that's politically incorrect. It's probably called Native American summer.

"All right," I said. "So what are the world's big questions?"

Andrew finished his cupcake and licked the frosting off his fingers. Then he said that the world's big questions are the ones that lead to an understanding of life, the universe, and everything.

Here are Andrew's big questions:

Is there life in outer space?

What was around before the Big Bang?

Why does time go forward but not backward?

Why can't we travel faster than the speed of light?

How do we talk to an alien if it's nothing like people but more like a jellyfish or a metal cube?

Is there really a Wealth Corner, and if I open my window to get a breath of fresh air because I am suffocating and dying of heat prostration, will the IRS really audit my parents' tax returns and bankrupt us so that we have to go live in Connecticut with my uncle Carl?

I thought those weren't bad actually, except the Wealth Corner one, which was sarcastic. Besides Andrew likes his uncle Carl.

"Why would anyone want to talk to a jellyfish?" I said.

"You would want to talk to it if it was an intelligent jellyfish," Andrew said. "Like a *Star Trek* jellyfish."

"There weren't any *Star Trek* jellyfish," I said. "On *Star Trek*, every intelligent alien life-form in the universe was like people."

"No, they weren't," said Andrew.

Looking shifty, so you could tell he couldn't think of any examples.

Then Aaron Pennebaker came over and told us about how his cousin Michael got stung on the leg by a jellyfish while he was swimming in the ocean in Hawaii.

"His leg swelled up and turned black, and they had to take him to the hospital," Aaron said. "He nearly died."

"Was it an intelligent jellyfish?" I said.

"No," said Aaron. "It was a stupid jellyfish. Michael is a jerk. A smart jellyfish would have stung him on the head."

Then the bell rang and we all had to go in.

*   *   *

Usually when I got home from school, Boone was in his shed in the backyard, painting his masterpiece. But that afternoon he was in the kitchen making dinner, though he was still wearing his painting clothes, which were a sweatshirt with the sleeves cut off and a pair of splattered overalls. Boone always said that his whole career was painted on those overalls. His Blue Period, his Yellow Period, his Red and Green Period. There was even a Pink Period on his rear end, but that might just have been where he sat down in something.

Boone did most of the cooking at our house, because Ray worked long hours at her law office and didn't have time. I liked Boone cooking, because it always gave us a chance to talk. When he was out in his shed, painting his masterpiece, he never liked to be disturbed because that broke his creative flow. But cooking didn't seem to require as much creative flow, or at least not the same kind.

I also liked it when I got to help. Boone would let me chop vegetables and grate cheese, and he taught me how to separate eggs. Though at first he told me that that's when you put one egg in the kitchen and one in the living room. I let him think I thought that was funny.

Then he showed me how you crack the egg and tip the yolk back and forth between the two halves of the shell until the white part drips into one bowl, and then you drop the yolk into another.

"Do you think there's a purpose to life?" I asked Boone.

"Is this a trick question?" Boone said.

"I don't think so," I said.

Boone began to heat olive oil in a frying pan while he considered.

From the back I could see where he'd gotten paint in his ponytail.

"I think the purpose of life is to make the most of it while you've got it," Boone said. "Because, in my opinion, we only get to go around once."

He threw some onion slices into the olive oil.

Then he said, "'You must live in the present, launch yourself on every wave, find your eternity in each moment.' That's Henry. Henry pretty much knows it all."

Henry is Henry David Thoreau. Boone always calls him Henry, as if Henry were still alive and living down the street and they were best buddies. He acts as if he and Henry sat on the porch together and kicked around the simple life and talked about the weather at Walden Pond and the best way to grow beans.

"So what do you think are the world's big questions?" I said.

Boone thought for a minute, stirring.

"The big one for me is 'Why won't your mother wear belly shirts?'" he said. "I think she'd look really good in one of those skimpy little shirts. And I ask her and she says, 'Don't be silly.' You could help me out there, Octavia. You could drop a hint. Get some advice from that fashion-nut friend of yours, the one who wants to be Coco Chanel."

"No, really," I said.

Boone threw some chopped peppers in with the onions and stirred some more.

"Seriously?" he said.

"Yeah, seriously," I said.

Boone thought again.

Then he said, "I think the world's biggest question is 'What is a good life?' It's the most important thing anybody has to solve."

"Well, what *is* a good life?" I said.

"Nobody can answer that for you," Boone said. "You have to work it out for yourself."

That means that Boone hasn't worked it out yet.

These are what I think are the world's big questions:

Is there a God?

If there is a God, then why do bad things happen to good people, like earthquakes and Hurricane Katrina and 9/11?

If there is a God, which religion is the right religion?

Do people have souls or just brains?

What happens to us after we die?

Is there a purpose to life?

Why would God bother to find math homework for dorks like Marjean?

CHAPTER 6

AFTER A FEW interminable Sundays with the Redeemers, I had learned a lot more about the kids in my class than I had ever wanted to know, and I had worked out a plan for running away from home and living in the Wolverton County Natural History Museum, in the diorama that had the bear cave. I figured I could have a pillow in there, and a flashlight so that I could read, and I could sneak out at night and get food out of the snack machines.

I knew the most about Marjean, because I was still sitting next to her and because Marjean planned to be a missionary someday to Zimbabwe or maybe the Amazon jungle in Brazil and she was treating me as a sort of practice heathen. Marjean's last name was Duveen. Marjean Duveen. She had two little brothers named Bud and Grover, and her dad drove a milk truck, one of those big tankers that goes around collecting milk from farms. Her mother stayed at home and scrubbed stuff. That's God's design, Marjean said. The man is the head of the house, just like God is the head of the church, and a woman's place is to serve the family in the home. I wondered if any of the Redeemers had spilled that to Ray, about serving the family in the home.

Marjean wanted to learn how to play the guitar because, along with being a missionary, she also wanted to be a Christian country-music star. Though my take was that she didn't have a snowball's chance in hell unless she traded in those frumpy dresses for a pair of rhinestone jeans.

I'd been wondering how Marjean survived the teasing at school, what with those braids and always wearing outfits that looked like they came out of the Sears, Roebuck catalog from 1895. But it turned out that she didn't go to public school. The Redeemers had their own school. Everybody in Mrs. Prescott's class went to it except me and Ronnie, who had learning disabilities and went to a special academy on the other side of town.

Ronnie lived in the trailer park over past the railroad tracks and his mother worked part-time at Tinker's Tavern on Main Street, but in the part of the tavern that serves the hamburgers, not the part that has the bar.

Cathy Ann used to be very fat, but she lost weight with the help of God, and now she was a size five.

Matthew wanted to go to college, but his parents didn't think much of college.

Todd wanted to make computer games with Christian superheroes, like David and Goliath, but with rocket guns.

Marie's grandmother once saw the face of Jesus Christ in a potato chip.

I'd done everything I could think of to get out of going back to the Fellowship of the Redeemer, including faking diphtheria and threatening suicide.

But Ray wasn't having any. Ray, once she got an idea in her head, was as stubborn as sixteen mules and the Rock of Gibraltar. I suppose that's what made her such a good lawyer, but it's not so great in a parent. Sometimes talking to Ray was like shouting down a well.

Boone wasn't any help either because he figured, what with Ray always switching around all the time, that all I had to do was wait a little bit and the whole thing would go away. Also he was obsessed with his latest masterpiece. He'd just head out to his painting shed saying "Try to be patient, Octavia, and don't nag and upset your mother."

"What about not upsetting *me*?" I said.

Yelled, actually.

But by then Boone was shut up in his shed and in the middle of creative flow, and might as well have been in a submarine at the bottom of the sea.

So I went next door to see Mr. and Mrs. Peacock.

Mr. and Mrs. Peacock are the closest thing I have to a grandfather and grandmother, since Boone is alienated from his parents due to irreconcilable philosophical differences and Ray's mother died before I was born. Her father is remarried and lives in Palm Beach with his second wife, Edna, who has blue hair and a wicked golf swing. They send a ten-dollar bill for my birthday and a check for Christmas, and that's about all I hear from them.

Anyway, as long as we've lived here, whenever Boone and Ray weren't around, I was sent next door to stay with the Peacocks. That worked out pretty well, since Mr. and Mrs. Peacock don't have any grandchildren of their own, due to Sandy having what Mr. Peacock says are shortsighted and unnatural career ambitions and no regard for biology. Mrs. Peacock likes children, and Mr. Peacock says I'm not as tomfool as most kids these days.

Mr. Peacock hadn't heard of the Redeemers, but he knew a lot about the Cadillac Motel because of the trouble Arnold Sykes got into there with that floozy half his age in a skirt the size of a penny postage stamp and hair of a color that nature never put on any woman, and him, Mr. Sykes, a respectable married man and a Grand Regent of the Loyal Order of the Moose, though what he had to put up with from Lucille Sykes afterward is something he, Mr. Peacock, wouldn't wish on a mongrel dog.

He would have said more, but Mrs. Peacock told him to hush.

Mrs. Peacock had heard of the Redeemers, due to believing in keeping informed about current events, unlike some people she could name, and reading something in the paper every day other than the sports page and the obituaries.

"They're not bad folks," she said. "They made a donation to the Fire Department Rescue Fund, even though some of them had objections to the way the station has those Saturday night bingo games. And they brought a whole lot of food for the potluck supper. One lady made a real nice macaroni and cheese."

Mr. Peacock made a snort like a rhinoceros, which I recognized from watching nature shows on TV, and said it was a sad world when people were ready to sell their principles down the river for a plate of macaroni and cheese.

"Well, what do you think I should do?" I said.

Mrs. Peacock looked up from where she was slicing applesauce cake.

"Well, Octavia, I don't see as you should do a thing," she said. "Your mama is a fine person, but she's flighty. So you can wear yourself and everybody else out making a lot of fuss and hullabaloo, or you can sit quiet and tight and wait till she flits off onto something else, which my guess is shouldn't take too long. And in the meantime a little Bible reading never hurt anybody."

"Don't be a tomfool, Clara Jane," Mr. Peacock said. "What they've got going on at that motel is a cult, and you know as well as me what to do when you meet up with a cult."

"What do you do when you meet up with a cult?" I said. I wondered if there were rules for cults like there were rules for other disasters. Like you're supposed to stand in a doorway during earthquakes and go to the cellar during tornadoes and get off the telephone during thunderstorms.

Mrs. Peacock set the applesauce cake on the table. Mr. Peacock forked up a big piece and put it on my plate. Then he pointed a bony finger at my nose.

"What you do when you meet up with a cult," he said, "is you get your young ass out of there."

We were having tea in the kitchen, which is my favorite room in the Peacock house, even though Boone says that from an artist's point of view it's a nightmare, like what might happen if Grandma Moses somehow got crossed up with Jasper Johns. The woodwork is turquoise, and the wallpaper has a pattern of big pink salt and pepper shakers. There's a shelf above the stove where Mrs. Peacock keeps her collection of teapots, including my favorite, that's shaped like a gingerbread cottage, and a framed certificate on the wall from when Mr. Peacock was honored by the Rotary Club, and a rocking chair, and a table with a red-and-white-checked oilcloth cover. I think it feels good. It has what Andrew's mom would call positive *chi*.

I put a lot of sugar and skim milk in my tea, which turned it into what Mrs. Peacock said was called cambric tea when she was a little girl.

Mr. Peacock said there is only one name for a drink with skim milk in it: swill.

"Well, I like it," I said.

Because Mr. Peacock is not completely trust-worthy when it comes to food.

Then we talked about the world's big questions. These are Mrs. Peacock's big questions:

Why did the Lord God see fit to make things like black flies and the common cold and other aggravations to the spirit?

Why do the people with the emptiest heads always have the loudest mouths?

And what possesses Claudine Boucher, who doesn't have the sense God gave a sick chicken, to think that she has anything to say about the operation of the Public Library Volunteer Circle, of which Mrs. Peacock has been president for the last fifteen years?

These are Mr. Peacock's big questions:

Why does the great American public always send such empty-headed tomfools to Washington, D.C., where they do nothing

*but sit around on their rumps and crank up
the price of pipe tobacco and gasoline?*

*If those psychics you see on TV are so psychic,
why don't they ever seem to know a damn
thing?*

*Why would anybody in their right mind buy
water in a tomfool plastic bottle when you
can get all the water you want right out of
the kitchen faucet?*

*And what's with those tight bicycle shorts
that anybody that wears them is squeezing
off the blood to the body in unnatural ways
and doing God knows what permanent
harm to a person's manly parts?*

He had more, but Mrs. Peacock hushed him up.

Mr. and Mrs. Peacock don't have any questions about the existence of God. They're convinced that he's there. They're also certain that after they die, which Mrs. Peacock refers to as Passing On, they'll go to heaven, where they'll be reunited with all their lost loved ones.

Mrs. Peacock says that while no one can presume to know the face of God, she's always imagined him as a wise old man with a white beard, a long white robe, and a shepherd's crook, like you sometimes see on the cover of the *Baptist Women's Quarterly Magazine.* Mr. Peacock said that in his mind, God looks pretty much like Abraham Lincoln, but without the stovepipe hat.

The one thing Mrs. Peacock isn't sure about is whether or not people are descended from apes, but Mr. Peacock says it's pretty obvious to him. He told Mrs. Peacock just to look at her brother Billy.

When I got home, there was a note on the refrigerator saying that Ray had gone to a Redeemers' meeting, and Boone was still in his shed.

These are my *O* words for that day: *Oppressed, IgnOred,* and *Overruled.*

And here's where I wanted to be: Oolloo Crossing. It's got five *O*s in it and it's in Australia, which is ten thousand miles away from Winton Falls.

CHAPTER 7

ANOTHER MONTH WENT BY and Ray didn't show any signs of flitting off onto something else. She liked the Redeemers.

I kept thinking about the life cycle of corals, how they begin as this little swimming thing called a planula that paddles all over looking for a good place to settle down. Then once it finally decides to settle, that's it. It sticks. It stays stuck to that place for the rest of its life and develops into a coral reef. It was like that for Ray. She'd paddled around all over the place, but once she paddled up to the Redeemers, she settled down and stuck.

She joined the Redeemers' Wednesday night Bible discussion group and prayer circle. She stopped wearing her gold-chain necklace and her earrings and even her wedding ring because the Redeemers don't believe in jewelry, because of the sin of vanity. She started keeping a Bible on her bedside table. She began getting a lot of phone calls from people I didn't know.

I couldn't understand why Boone didn't care.

"Doesn't it bother you how Ray is off with the Redeemers all the time?" I said.

Boone shook his head.

"Don't worry so much," he said. "Give her some space. She'll drop them any day now. You know your mom. These things don't last very long with her."

I began to feel sorry for Boone, because there's a lot you miss when you're out in the yard shut up in a shed. Boone was like an ostrich with his head buried, but in oil paint, not in sand. I realized suddenly how much of the time Boone basically wasn't there.

Then one night he finally yanked out his head and looked up.

We were eating dinner, the three of us together, which we didn't do very often due to Ray's crowded schedule with her clients at the law office and Boone's creative flow. Since those times were special, we always used the Mexican tablecloth that Boone and Ray got in Mexico City on their honeymoon and put flowers on the table. That night I'd picked chrysanthemums from Boone's garden and arranged them in a big glass jar. I love chrysanthemums, first because *chrysanthemum* is such a great fluffy orange-Popsicle-colored word, and second because of the spelling-lesson scene in *Anne of Green Gables*, where Anne beats Gilbert Blythe by spelling it: "Chrysanthemum. C-H-R-Y-S-A-N-T-H-E-M-U-M. Chrysanthemum."

Unfortunately I have never had this word on a spelling test.

Dinner was cheese ravioli and green salad with tomatoes and cucumbers and black olives, except not on mine because the word *olive* reminds me of a rubber ball, which is also what I think black olives taste like. Boone and Ray each had a glass of red wine. The Redeemers don't believe in drinking coffee or tea, because those aren't in the Bible, but wine is okay because of the Wedding at Cana and the Last Supper, provided it is taken in moderation.

Usually I looked forward to those special dinners. We'd all catch each other up about what we were doing, and Boone would make his feeble jokes and we'd laugh, and we'd all sit around together and not just jump up right off to clear the plates. I liked it because I thought that was how family dinners ought to be. I think Boone and Ray did too, even though they'd tease about Mom's apple pie and Norman Rockwell and the Waltons.

But that's not what it was like this time. This dinner didn't feel right at all. Boone and Ray weren't eating much, or talking much either, and when they did talk, they said things like "How are you?" and "Fine," like people who don't know each other very well but run into each other at bus stops.

After a while it was so uncomfortable that I was just wishing the meal would be over so that I could go upstairs to my room and get back to *Anne of Windy Poplars,* which is book four of the Anne of Green Gables series. There are eight books in all, starting with *Anne of Green Gables* and ending with *Rilla of Ingleside.*

Then Boone threw down his chopsticks so that they bounced off the Mexican tablecloth and onto the floor. Boone always ate with chopsticks because he'd read in *The Good Life* by Scott and Helen Nearing, who were homesteaders in Vermont for about a hundred years and grew all their own food, that they always ate with chopsticks out of wooden bowls. Ray used to tease him all the time about those chopsticks.

"I don't get this," Boone said. "I don't *get* this, Rachel. Could you just please explain to me what's going on all of a sudden with you and this Redeemer thing?"

"I'm not sure I can," Ray said.

"Well, *try*," Boone said, sounding impatient and exasperated, like he does when somebody bangs on his shed door when he's in the middle of creative flow.

"Stop *yelling*, Simon," Ray said.

"I'm *not* yelling," Boone said. "I just really want to understand."

I just really wanted to go upstairs.

"I don't think I can explain," Ray said. "It's something that just happens. You don't think it through. It comes to you. You feel it."

Right off I thought about *Star Wars: The Phantom Menace*, where the Jedi knight tells Luke Skywalker's father to just feel, not think. I always thought that was lousy advice. For example, if you're flying a spaceship and zipping along at about a million miles a minute, you ought to be thinking, not feeling.

"I've always felt sort of empty," Ray said. "Like nothing really meant anything. You know what I mean, Simon. You've said it too. Think how most people live. They run around all the time working at their jobs so they can make enough money to buy a car and a flat-screen TV and maybe take a vacation every once in a while and go to Disneyland."

Actually I'd always wanted to go to Disneyland. Andrew's family went last year, and Andrew said it was really cool except that his little sister Amanda made everybody crazy because she wouldn't get out of the giant teacups.

"Is that all there is?" Ray said. "Is that what life's all about? I was standing in the office parking lot looking at bumper stickers the other day. Just standing there looking at bumper stickers. SHOP-AHOLIC. SHOP UNTIL YOU DROP. WHOEVER DIES WITH THE MOST TOYS WINS. And I thought, *This is sick*."

"You mean you think we've got too much stuff?" Boone said.

"I'm not talking about *things*," Ray said. "I'm talking about what really matters. I'm talking about how people spend all their time running around on these daily little hamster wheels and then one day they die. There's no point to it. No real purpose."

"I don't know what you mean by purpose," Boone said. "I think what it's all about is finding a person you love, raising kids, doing work you find rewarding, and maybe trying to leave the planet in a little better shape than you found it. That's purpose enough for me. Isn't that important?"

"Of course it's important," Ray said. "But there has to be more to it than that. The only way it all makes any sense is if there's something bigger than us. Better than us. It only makes sense if there's God. If the purpose of life is to know and serve God. That's what I believe."

"Give me a break, Ray," Boone said.

Ray leaned forward.

"The Redeemers really have answers," Ray said. "They're the most honest people I've ever known, and the most sincere. Just by being what they are, they've helped me believe too. I finally found what I've been missing out on, what I've been looking for even though I didn't really know I was looking. It's a revelation. It's like the Bible says: 'For now we see through a glass, darkly, but then face to face.'"

She put down her fork, but neatly, on her plate.

Boone stared at her.

I thought about looking through a glass darkly. I thought it would be like the black filters Andrew and I once used to look at a solar eclipse. Which you couldn't look at face to face without burning out your eyeballs.

I thought suddenly that maybe Ray had looked at the Redeemers face to face and they'd burned out her brain.

"And I pray all the time that you and Octavia will come to believe too. I've never known anything like this before. I love this feeling. I love the person I'm becoming. It's like everything finally fell into place. It's wonderful."

It didn't seem so wonderful to me.

But I also knew that once people start talking about feelings and love, there is no point in trying to reason with them. Infatuated people have lost all sense of proportion. I thought of Andrew and his eight-week one-sided romance with Julie Laroche, during which he was such a brainless puddle of butter that if Julie had had the wit to ask him, he would have signed over his college fund.

I looked at Ray across the table.

Don't feel, I thought. *Think.*

"Listen to yourself, Ray," Boone said. "Just listen to yourself. This isn't you. This isn't the person I married. Something's happened to you. I think you need help."

"This *is* me," Ray said. "And something *has* happened to me. That's what I've been telling you, Simon, but you haven't been listening. I don't think you've been listening all along."

Angelique Soulier says that when her parents fight, they scream at each other in French and her mother throws plates, and then everybody cries and hugs and sweeps up the mess and makes up. I suddenly wished that Ray would scream and throw things instead of just sitting there sounding so reasonable and untouchable. I wished most of all that she and Boone would cry and hug and make up.

"Whatever you're feeling, Rachel," Boone said, "I can guarantee it's not God. I think you need to stop thinking about God and think about your family for a change. And I think most of all that you need to get away from the crazies at that damn motel and go see a psychiatrist."

Then he put down his wineglass hard, so that some of the wine slopped out onto the table, and shoved back his chair and got up and walked out of the room. Then we heard the back door slam and when I looked out the window, I could see that the lights had come on in his shed.

"What if he's right?" I said.

"You know nothing about it, Octavia," Ray said, in her I-am-not-going-to-discuss-this-with-the-child voice.

I hate that voice.

"That's what you think," I said.

"That's enough of that tone, Octavia," Ray said.

Being a Redeemer had made Ray cold and reasonable with Boone and critical and snappy with me. Ray had always been gone a lot, on account of having a demanding job, but we'd always gotten along just fine. She used to stick funny notes for me on the refrigerator, and instead of signing her name, she would draw this silly little face with hair that stuck up all around like porcupine quills. Sometimes she would leave surprises for me on the kitchen table, like peppermint Life Savers or leopard-print socks or a book she thought I'd like to read. But now everything was changing.

I think by then the Redeemers had been getting at her about her and Boone's child-rearing practices. She started quoting this Bible verse all the time: "Train up a child in the way he should go: and when he is old, he will not depart from it."

Now practically every word I said, Ray thought it was talking back.

Here's another big question.

> *What makes a more-or-less normal person*
> *with a more-or-less normal life suddenly go*
> *off the deep end about God?*

I haven't much liked cheese ravioli since.

My *O* word for that day was *Opalling*, until I found out that it's actually spelled with an *A*.

CHAPTER 8

ANDREW SAID THAT Ray had snapped.

He read an article about snapping at the library in an old issue of *Psychology Today* while he was waiting for his little sister Amanda, who was researching the solar system. Amanda was in third grade. Her class was studying outer space, and for the science fair, she was planning to make a solar system model out of vegetables.

"It's like brainwashing," Andrew said.

He put a handful of Goldfish crackers in his mouth. As I said, Andrew is always eating something. My theory is that he has the metabolism of a hummingbird, and if he goes for more than ten seconds without food, he'll die.

"It's how cults recruit people. They're all nice and friendly and they pay you all kinds of attention and they talk at you and talk at you, until suddenly you just snap and then you're a cult member. You can't think of anything else. Your brain chemistry changes and everything."

Andrew stuck his hands out in front of him and went stalking across the floor like the zombies in *Night of the Living Dead.*

I didn't think it was funny. I was mad at Ray for causing all this trouble, but I didn't want her ending up a zombie.

Andrew ate another handful of Goldfish crackers, thus prolonging his existence for another ten seconds.

"But you can unbrainwash them," Andrew said. "Parents do it all the time when it happens to their kids."

"How?" I said.

I was willing.

"First they kidnap the kids," Andrew said. "They hire people to steal them away from the cult. Sometimes they raid the cult headquarters in the middle of the night and grab them. Then they take them someplace and lock them up and deprogram them."

"How do they do that?" I said.

"I only skimmed that part," Andrew said. "Because Amanda was in my face and kept asking if I thought Jupiter should be a cabbage and Saturn a head of iceberg lettuce or the other way around. But it sounded like you just keep asking them logical questions until they realize how screwed up they've been, and then they snap back to normal again."

I should have known it wasn't going to be that simple, though, because of what happened at Halloween.

First I have to say that I love Halloween.

I even love the word *Halloween*, which I always see as sort of smooth and stripy, with a hard shiny shell like a pumpkin or an acorn squash. I love going out in the dark when the air has that spicy fall smell and the dead leaves crackle when you walk on them and there are jack-o'-lanterns lit on all the porches. The bare black tree branches look wild and witchy, and on clear nights the sky is thick with stars. We see a lot of stars in Winton Falls because we don't have much light pollution due to the streetlights being all about a hundred years old and lit with two-watt bulbs.

Andrew and I always trick-or-treat together. I wear different costumes every year, but Andrew is always a robot, except for our first year together, the year we were in kindergarten, when his mother forced him to be a teddy bear.

Last year he had a robotic arm that he built with the motor from his old Erector set, that had a retractable claw that he used to pick up his candy. The year before that, he had a backpack made of plastic soda bottles with flashlight bulbs inside so that when he pushed a button, he glowed green. This year he was making an outfit out of paper-towel tubes covered with aluminum foil, with a hidden recording of a mechanical voice that said, "Feed me, Seymour."

That's a line from the movie *Little Shop of Horrors*, which is about a giant carnivorous plant from an alien planet.

I was going as a penguin. I had made my costume from an old white sweatshirt of Ray's and a black jacket that used to belong to Boone. I had a black baseball cap for my head, and an orange cardboard beak that tied behind my ears and orange cardboard feet. I even had an egg that I'd made with a balloon and instant papier-mâché.

On the Sunday before Halloween, this is what Mrs. Prescott wrote on the blackboard in my Redeemer classroom:

> There shall not be found among you any one that maketh his son or his daughter to pass through the fire, or that useth divination, or an observer of times, or an enchanter, or a witch, or a charmer, or a consulter with familiar spirits, or a wizard, or a necromancer.
>
> For all that do these things are an abomination unto the Lord: and because of these abominations

the Lord thy God doth drive them out from before thee.

— DEUTERONOMY 18:10–12

"What's that all about?" I asked Marjean, trying to think of what kind of circumstance would make you want to pass your son or daughter through a fire. Maybe if you were escaping from a burning house, in which case it seemed like it should be an "absolutely should" rather than a "shall not."

Marjean was wearing a black cardigan sweater and a red calico dress that hung down practically to her ankles. I wondered where her mother got her awful clothes.

"It's a warning about Halloween," Marjean said. "We don't celebrate it because it's a glorification of the works of Satan."

"You've got to be kidding," I said. I mean, come on.

"Last year on Halloween we had a House of Sins here in the church," Cathy Ann said. "It started in the lobby and went through all the classrooms. Pastor Bruno dressed up as the devil and he had a fan with strips of red cellophane for flames. A lot of the parents did all the different sins. You had to be over ten years old to see some parts of it."

"That sounds a lot worse than just plain Halloween," I said.

"Well, it wasn't," Marjean said. "It was about forswearing the devil and all his works."

Margarine, I thought.

"When Mrs. Prescott comes in, she's going to ask us all to resist temptation on Halloween," Marjean said. "She's going to ask us to promise to come to the prayer meeting here instead."

"Well, I'm not going to promise," I said.

I wanted to be a penguin.

"Well, you go right ahead," Marjean said. "But if you don't promise, you'll go to hell."

All that must have gotten right back to Ray, because the next thing I knew there was another fight at home.

"Aren't you getting too old for Halloween?" Ray said.

Which was her sideways way of trying to talk me out of it without bringing up the Redeemers.

"Louanne Pelletier says that Polly hasn't trick-or-treated for two years now. Neither has Sara Boudreau."

I said, "I've got my costume all ready."

"Oh, come on, Ray," Boone said. "She's not too old yet. You're not too old as long as you're still having fun."

"Maybe that kind of fun isn't such a good idea," Ray said.

"What's that supposed to mean?" said Boone.

Ray started fooling with her hair, twisting it around her fingers, which she does when she knows there's about to be an argument.

"I just mean that maybe we never put enough thought into it," Ray said. "About what it all really represents."

"So what does it all really represent?" Boone said, sounding ominous.

"It's not really wholesome, is it?" Ray said. "Getting all these kids thinking about witchcraft and the Devil."

"Oh, Christ," Boone said, which made Ray sort of wince. "It's *Halloween*. It's not some sinister satanic plot, Ray. It's just a bunch of kids dressing up and running around in the dark. She's going to be a *penguin,* for God's sake."

"You know there's more to it than that, Simon," Ray said, tightening up her lips like she does when she's angry, but trying not to lose her temper.

"No," Boone said, getting louder like he does when he's angry and doesn't care whether he loses his temper or not. "No, Ray, I *don't* know that there's more to it than that. I don't believe in witchcraft. What I think is that our daughter is going out with her friend to get some of Clara Peacock's popcorn balls, of which I hope she gets at least two, so she can bring one home to me. I think what you're thinking is nuts, Rachel, and I wish to hell you'd snap out of it."

Snap back, I thought, and I crossed my fingers.

But Ray didn't.

She and Boone just stood there glaring at each other across the room

Then Ray said, "Have it your way, Simon. But I'll be praying for you, Octavia, and you know that I love you, and if you change your mind, you know we want to have you with us."

And I got a cold feeling in my stomach.

Because by *us,* she didn't mean her and Boone.

This pretty much ruined Halloween.

There are some things that can't be fixed even by Mrs. Peacock's popcorn balls.

CHAPTER 9

ANDREW HAD LOTS OF plans for kidnapping Ray.

First he thought that we should write a letter, luring her to an isolated spot like the back parking lot of Menard's Grocery & Liquor Store, and then when she showed up, we'd pounce on her from behind, bundle her into a car, and drive away. Then he thought we could do a commando raid, showing up at her office disguised in ski masks, dropping a blanket over her head, and whisking her off down the back stairs. None of these plans seemed very sensible to me, first because there was a security guard at Ray's office, and second because neither of us knew how to drive, even though Andrew claimed he did, due to experience with his father's riding lawn mower.

Also it wasn't clear to me what we'd do with Ray once we got her. Ray had changed.

I read about this bush from West Africa that has little red berries that are called miracle berries because after you eat them, they make everything sour taste sweet. That's what Ray was like, like she'd eaten miracle berries and now nothing was like the way it had been before. It was as if she was off in a whole new world, with lemons suddenly as sweet as maple sugar. And you could say, "Hey, those things are sour enough to shrivel your tongue," over and over until you turned blue, but to her it didn't taste like that, so she didn't believe you.

With Ray turned into a religious maniac and Boone practically living in his shed, I found that I really missed Priscilla. Which I know sounds dumb, but there are times in your life when you really need an understanding friend, even if it's an invisible one with flippers. That doesn't mean Andrew isn't a great friend, because he is, but this was different.

I kept thinking how nice it used to be when Priscilla slept in my bed, and how I used to imagine the two of us wearing matching pajamas, and how Priscilla was afraid of the dark but I didn't mind asking for a night-light as long as it was for her. I used to tell her all my problems and my secrets, and she always knew just what I was talking about and she always agreed with me.

In the future, Andrew says, there will be robots who do this for us.

Then I thought about Ray's weird new relationship with God. Maybe Ray had needed a Priscilla too, I thought. Maybe that's what she was getting from the Redeemers: an invisible friend who always supported her and understood everything she had to say. *Who wouldn't want that?* I thought.

On the other hand, even though I wouldn't ever admit it to anybody at the time, and I still don't, I always knew, deep down, that Priscilla wasn't real.

At school in Winton Falls, everybody was beginning to obsess over the science fair. Even though it was still months away, we had to hand in our plans in advance, which I think was because of Mr. Clover Harrison still being mad about the cabbage.

Polly Pelletier's science-fair project was titled "The Chemistry of the Permanent Wave." On a Monday, the day that her mother's Creative Clip Shoppe was closed, Polly was going to try out different combinations of permanent chemicals on five of us and then put photographs of the results on a poster showing what it takes to make hair curly. I was Subject #3, and I knew I was going to give Polly a run for her money since my hair is straight as a board.

Sara Boudreau was Subject #1. Polly and Sara's friendship was back on track again, since all of a sudden they both showed up in class wearing purple leggings and purple plaid tops and purple headbands and gold-flecked purple nail polish.

Jean-Claude Chevalier's project was on crime-scene investigation. Jean-Claude is a fan of *CSI*. He was making blood-splatter patterns with his brother's paintball gun.

Aaron Pennebaker was making a model of the radioactive spider that turned Peter Parker into Spider-Man.

Angelique Soulier was evaluating what kind of nutrients belong in the ideal hamster diet. Her name on her project was going to appear as Jennifer, because she thought it was time her family started getting used to the idea.

Celeste Olavson was soaking chicken bones in vinegar and then tying them into knots, which was meant to show the importance of calcium in the diet and the future benefits of physical therapy.

Nobody knew yet what Andrew was going to do because he still wouldn't tell, and Ms. Hodges wouldn't either, due to respecting confidentiality.

And I still hadn't made up my mind.

Then I found out that there was a science fair at the Redeemers' school too, because the next Sunday, when Ray forced me to go to class, even though I explained how the Constitution banned cruel and unusual punishment, which this was, and the Supreme Court would have backed me up, all the science projects were on display on tables in the lobby. Everybody in Mrs. Prescott's class had an entry, except me and Ronnie, whose special academy does not do science fairs.

It wasn't like any science fair I'd ever seen, since the projects all had titles like "Evidence for Noah's Flood" and "On the Sixth Day, God Created Horses" and "Apples: Botany in the Garden of Eden." Under each title there was a quotation from the Bible.

At the middle-grade level, Paul won first prize and Marjean got an honorable mention.

Paul's project was called "The Origin of Life," and his Bible quotation was "And God said, Let the waters bring forth abundantly the moving creature that hath life, and fowl that may fly above the earth in the open firmament of heaven" (Genesis 1:20).

What Paul did was put all the ingredients of life in a mason jar. He crushed a charcoal briquette for carbon and ground up a multivitamin pill for minerals and nutrients, and then he mixed it all up with boiled water. Then he left the jar on his bedroom windowsill in the sun for two months. Then he looked at the water under a microscope to see if any life had developed, and it hadn't. His conclusion was that life could only appear if there is a miraculous intervention by God.

The jar was there, full of gray muddy water, and Paul had a microscope set up so that you could look and see that there was nothing alive in it.

Marjean's project was called "Adam's Help Meet: A Woman's Place," and her Bible quotation was "But I would have you know, that the head of every man is Christ; and the head of the woman is the man; and the head of Christ is God" (I Corinthians 11:3). Her exhibit was a poster showing how God designed women to be housewives and mothers. She had pictures of pelvises, showing how women's are different from men's and specially suited for carrying babies, and a chart showing how women aren't as good as men at math and science, which proves that God didn't give them the sort of logical minds that would allow them to do either, and a graph showing how women don't make as much money as men in the workplace, which proves that God doesn't want them to work outside the home. She also had a lot of cassette tapes of interviews with women who had quit jobs, and all of them said they were much happier now that they were where God wanted them to be.

I thought they were pretty lousy experiments.

I looked around for Ray, because no matter what kind of revelation Ray had had, I *knew* she wouldn't agree about women being Adam's Help Meet. All the time I'd been growing up, she'd always been telling me that I could do anything if I set my mind to it and not to ever let anybody make me believe that I couldn't. Ray was in favor of the Equal Rights Amendment. Back when she was in college, she marched in parades and burned her bra. But Ray wasn't anywhere in sight.

And it was right then that I got my brilliant idea for the school science fair. I realized that if I could convince Ray through science that the Redeemers were all wrong, she'd have to stop believing and snap back to how she was before. And I'd thought of a way of getting incontrovertible proof. If I believed in revelations, I would have said that I'd had a revelation, except that would have meant that God was showing me how to prove that there is no God.

This was my hypothesis: If there is a God, prayer must work.

Here are some of the things different people say prayer cures: high blood pressure, heart attacks, tumors, and ulcers. They also claim that prayer keeps bacteria from growing, which helps people fight off infections. It makes wounds heal faster, and it boosts people out of depression and keeps them from committing suicide. On the other hand, a scientist named Sir Francis Galton, who lived in the nineteenth century and invented a lot of stuff like fingerprinting and the dog whistle, said that he had evidence that prayer didn't work at all. Galton said that in spite of everybody in England constantly saying "God save the king!" or "God save the queen!" which made the king and queen the most prayed-for people in the country, kings and queens didn't live any longer than anybody else. Some of them even ended up with their heads chopped off.

So here's what I decided to pray for: beans. I thought that was a nice touch, seeing as Boone's pal Henry David Thoreau was always growing beans in his garden at Walden Pond.

I decided to plant eight pots of beans and treat

them all exactly alike, except that I'd pray for four of them, asking God to make them grow enormous like the magic beans in *Jack and the Beanstalk*. The other four, I'd spiritually ignore. I figured that if all my beans turned out pretty much the same, that would show that prayer didn't make any difference. And if prayer didn't make any difference, that would be absolute scientific proof that there wasn't any God. With scientific proof right there in front of her, Ray would have to give up the Redeemers and be normal again.

And it would answer the biggest of my big questions too.

My *O* words for that day were *Outmaneuver, Outwit,* and *Outsmart.* Because that's what I was so sure that I'd be able to do.

CHAPTER 10

HERE IS WHAT I FOUND in December, written by Mrs. Prescott on the board:

> Thus saith the Lord: Learn not the way of the heathen, and be not dismayed at the signs of heaven; for the heathen are dismayed at them. For the customs of the people are vain: for one cutteth a tree out of the forest, the work of the hands of the workman, with the axe. They deck it with silver and with gold; they fasten it with nails and with hammers, that it move not.
>
> —JEREMIAH 10:2–4

By now I could pretty much figure out where this was heading without any help from Marjean, but Marjean translated anyway.

"It's about Christmas," Marjean said. She was wearing her black cardigan, a long green wool skirt, and lumpy lace-up shoes that looked like combat boots.

She was going to say more, but I got there first.

"It's a pagan holiday and you don't celebrate it," I said, which made Marjean look crushed, but I didn't care.

By then, Ray was beginning to seem as alien as Andrew's intelligent jellyfish. It's one thing to give up Halloween, I thought, but how could anybody chuck Christmas? I thought of what a beautiful word *Christmas* was, like stained-glass windows and tinsel, and how Ray had always loved everything about it.

"There's nothing in the Bible that says December twenty-fifth has anything to do with the birth of our Lord," Marjean said.

Shut up, Margarine, I thought.

I couldn't believe Ray would give up Christmas. And I wasn't thinking about the presents either, not that those aren't fun and that there weren't a few things I wanted. I meant all our family things. Every family has them, no matter what holidays you celebrate: Christmas or Kwanzaa or Hanukkah, or something else that I haven't heard of. Andrew says that his parents are always threatening to celebrate Festivus, which is for people who are minimalists and don't like Christmas at all, so instead of a Christmas tree, they put up a plain pole in a bucket. But it never happens, because Andrew's mother is a sucker for Christmas. She bakes these cookies called moon pies and hangs lights on everything and puts red feng shui ribbons all over their Christmas tree.

Here's what Boone and Ray and I always do. We make gingerbread men and chocolate-covered orange peel, and Boone bakes a special Christmas cake with flattened-out gumdrops on it in the shape of a poinsettia or a star. We get our tree from Chevalier's Christmas Tree Farm—not Jean-Claude's farm, but his uncle Al's—and we cut it down ourselves and bring it home on top of the car, and Boone always says that it's too tall and will never fit in the house unless we cut a hole in the ceiling, but it always does and we never have to. Then we make paper chains and popcorn and cranberry strings to put on it, and we all have special ornaments. Ray has some from when she was a little girl: a Santa Claus and an angel with a gold halo and a sled with red letters on it that says RAY.

Boone reads all our Christmas books out loud every year on Christmas Eve, even though I've gotten way too old for some of them—*How the Grinch Stole Christmas* and *The Polar Express* and *A Christmas Carol*—and then late at night, like midnight, we bundle up and go for a night walk, all three of us, and every year Boone says that he hears reindeer hooves and the bells of Santa's sleigh.

"Shhh!" Boone says, and he holds up his hand, and then I play along and say that I hear hooves and bells too.

Then Ray starts to sing. She sings "O Holy Night," which is her favorite Christmas carol, and then Boone sings something called "Grandma Got Run Over by a Reindeer," which he claims is his.

"Mrs. Prescott is going to ask us to promise that we won't give in to the materialism of secular Christmas," Marjean said.

I thought that Marjean didn't know what she was talking about. I bet that she and Bud and Grover had never been taken for a night walk on Christmas Eve. I bet she and Bud and Grover wouldn't know a Christmas tradition if it bit them in the rear end.

"Your mom will be here with us because she's found God's grace," Marjean said. "I feel sorry for you and your dad."

Right then everything inside me just exploded. I felt like the Redeemers had taken those Christmas Eve walks that I always thought were so beautiful and holy and made them shallow and selfish and wrong.

"JUST SHUT UP!" I screamed, and I jumped out of my chair and grabbed Marjean with both hands by those long braids and tried to yank them right out of her head. Marjean shrieked at the top of her lungs and tried to kick me with her combat boots, but I wouldn't let go.

I was sort of hysterical.

It took Mrs. Prescott and Ronnie and Paul and the teacher from the eighth-grade room across the hall to pry us apart. Then Mrs. Prescott took Marjean, who was sobbing and clutching the top of her head, to the ladies' room, and I was sent to sit in the hall to wait for Ray.

I hoped I'd given Marjean a concussion or snatched her bald.

I hoped I'd disgraced Ray so much that the Redeemers would throw her out and never let her come back.

But they didn't.

The next thing that happened was that we had a family talk. That's what Ray called it, but by that time it was less of a talk than an announcement.

CHAPTER 11

HERE'S WHAT I THINK: people should not do irrevocable painful things on holidays. Because then the
holidays are never just holidays anymore. From then
on they're also anniversaries of awful events. Like
for Boone and me, Halloween is now the anniversary of when we first realized that Ray had turned
away from us. And now, as long as I live, even when
I'm grown up with kids of my own, even when I'm
old, I won't be able to think about Christmas the
way I did once, when I was really young. For me, it
will always be an anniversary.

We were all sitting in the living room, Boone and me on the blue plaid couch, the one about which Boone had said that he'd rather sit alone on a pumpkin, and Ray in the matching blue plaid easy chair. Outside it was snowing. What people called spitting snow. Just a few flakes every now and then falling down from a thick steel-colored sky. Everything was cold and gray. Nobody much was out except a couple of little kids down the street who were trying to make a snowman, but the snow didn't stick together very well, so then they just started chasing each other around. Everybody else was inside staying close to their woodstoves. The birds at the bird feeder were just sitting there with their feathers all fluffed up, trying to keep warm.

"I want you to know that this is really hard for me," Ray said.

Boone didn't say anything. I felt cold all the way through to my bones.

Ray took a deep breath and turned toward me.

"I've already talked to your father about this, Octavia," she said. "I'm giving up my law practice.

I've already told them at the office, and they've been very understanding. I'll be leaving as of the first of the year."

Ray started twisting her hair, so I knew there was more.

Then she said, all in a rush, "And I'm moving over to Wolverton, where I'm going to share a house with a couple of friends. I signed the lease early last week."

Boone looked shocked, like this was new to him too.

I felt like somebody had stabbed me in the stomach with an icicle.

"What friends?" I said. My voice sounded funny, like it was making words out of wires. "From the Redeemers?"

"Yes," Ray said. "I've made a commitment to the Redeemers. I'll be doing legal work for the church and helping with fund-raising campaigns. Eventually I'll be teaching. I think it's going to be a way of helping other people, and of helping myself at the same time."

I thought about my beans.

I'd planted them and they were sitting in a row on my bedroom windowsill, so far looking pretty much alike. They all had tiny little curved sprouts that looked like somebody had buried a pale-green paper clip.

I'd expanded the experiment by giving Mr. and Mrs. Peacock and Andrew Wochak's parents eight pots of beans too. Andrew's father, who was a Buddhist, was meditating for four of their beans, and Andrew's mother had tied red ribbons around the pots and was subjecting them to protective feng shui. Mrs. Peacock was offering Baptist prayers for four of their beans, but Mr. Peacock wasn't, since he said he wasn't about to hassle the Almighty over some tomfool vegetable.

What if I'm wrong? I thought. What if the prayed-for beans grow like maniacs and the not-prayed-for beans stay pitiful stunted twigs?

"You might have given us a chance to talk before just dropping it on me like this," Boone said.

"I've tried," Ray said. She had started to cry. Tears welled up behind her horn-rimmed glasses and rolled down her cheeks. "I've been trying to tell you for weeks. But you wouldn't listen to me."

"Ray, this is all a mistake," Boone said. He didn't sound angry, just sad. He talked soft and quiet, like people do when they're talking to an animal that's spooked and might take off running at any minute. "Why don't you give it a little more time? Why don't we go away for a weekend somewhere and talk? We can work this out. You know I love you."

Ray shook her head.

"It's different now, Simon," she said.

I'd always thought that Ray was a crisp white name, like cool clean sheets on summer nights or those old-fashioned starched nurse's caps with the curly brims. Now I thought maybe it was just cold, like ice and snow.

"What about Octavia?" Boone said.

Ray took off her glasses and mopped her eyes with her sleeve.

"I'll only be fifteen miles away," she said. "I want Octavia with me. As soon as I'm settled, we'll work out a schedule so that she can come on weekends to stay." She turned to me. "Then on Sundays I can take you to the Fellowship for your class."

"I don't want to go there anymore," I said.

I didn't add that they probably wouldn't have me, seeing as I'd tried to kill Marjean.

"Well, we'll see about that," Ray said.

Boone's face had gone stiff.

"You might have given me a little more notice, Rachel," he said again. "All these decisions you've been making have an impact, you know. It's not all about you."

"I'm sorry," Ray said. "I'm sorry it worked out this way. But I've thought about this a lot, and I know this is something I have to do."

It wasn't until later that it dawned on me what Ray had really said. With Ray working for the Redeemers and not her law office anymore, she wouldn't be making much money. And without Ray making money, nobody would be paying for our house and groceries and clothes and Boone's oil paints and all the other stuff we buy. So Boone wouldn't be able to work on his masterpiece anymore. He'd have to come out of his shed and get a job.

It only took Ray a couple of days to move out, so it was pretty clear she'd been planning this for a while. She didn't take much stuff with her to the Redeemers' house. She already had a lot of things packed up to give away, first because it's harder for a camel to go through a needle's eye than for a rich person to get into heaven, and second because the Redeemers do not believe in stuff like summer dresses with skinny shoulder straps and music that doesn't have Christian themes and DVDs that are rated anything over PG-13. She took some books and the rocking chair and a painting that Boone had made for her before they got married and the photo albums with all the pictures of me as a baby. It wasn't that much, but even so it made the house feel empty. There was nothing left in her closet when I looked in it but some dust bunnies and a bent hanger on the floor.

*   *   *

Boone and I went and cut the Christmas tree by ourselves, but it wasn't much fun without Ray, and Boone wasn't even making any of his feeble jokes, which I actually missed. We hiked through the crunchy snow in our boots, all muffled up with our heads down, and every once in a while one of us would look up and point at a tree and say, "What about that one?" and the other one of us would say, "No, crooked," or "No, too squatty." Then finally I said, "What about that one?" and Boone said, "Yeah, okay." It wasn't what you'd call festive.

Jean-Claude Chevalier's uncle Al gave us the tree for free, because he felt sorry for us, because as I said, this is a small town and everybody always knows everybody else's business. By then there wasn't a single kid at Winton Falls Elementary and Middle School K–8 who didn't know that Rachel Boone had quit her job, left home, and moved to Wolverton to live with the Jesus freaks.

I knew Andrew felt bad for me, but how he showed it was to talk a lot more than usual in order to distract me. It did distract me some, but not all that much.

Boone and I decorated our tree alone. I made a paper chain with red and green shiny paper, but we didn't string popcorn, because Ray was always best at that, and Boone had forgotten to get any cranberries. Then we hung the ornaments, but when we came to what used to be Ray's special box, with the Santa and the angel and the little sled that said RAY, Boone just sat down all of a sudden in the blue plaid chair and put his face in his hands.

I'd never seen Boone cry.

I wondered what it was like for Ray over in Wolverton without any Christmas tree at all.

In Winton Falls, it was a terrible Christmas.

CHAPTER **12**

AFTER THAT CAME an even lower point in my life.

Usually I love winter, which is a good thing given the latitude we live at, which is practically the North Pole. In the winter it gets dark before dinnertime, but it's cozy with the woodstove burning, and Boone makes cocoa—the really good kind that you simmer with milk in a pan. Jean-Claude Chevalier's uncle Al has horses and a sleigh, that we have rides on once the snow gets deep enough, bundled up under big scratchy plaid blankets that smell like a barn, and the town has a skating rink behind Menard's Grocery & Liquor Store.

There's a sledding hill too, on which Andrew and I once made a bobsled run by digging a sort of tunnel, hooking up five garden hoses in a row so that they'd reach, spraying the slope with water, and letting it freeze. It was great. I never thought it was fair that we got into so much trouble over it. I mean, Jody Boudreau was only seven, so those weren't his permanent teeth.

I liked it too that I got to see more of Boone in winter. His shed was cold.

Not last winter, though, because of the arrangement with Ray.

That is, Boone's arrangement with Ray. This is how it worked: during the school week I would stay with Boone and go to school. After school, if Boone was in his shed, I would stay with Mr. and Mrs. Peacock. Every Friday I would get shipped into Wolverton to sleep on the daybed in the house that Ray shared with two other Redeemers named Alda and Geraldine.

I hated the arrangement and I didn't like Alda and Geraldine and they didn't like me. Though I have to say that under other circumstances I might have found them kind of cool. Geraldine was tall and thin and elegant, with perfect teeth and the sort of legs you see on fashion models and movie stars, at least below the knees. She worked at a psychological counseling service for troubled teens. Alda was short and cushiony and coffee-colored. She ran a community kitchen that made meals for disabled people and senior citizens. They were polite to me and everything, and you could tell they really liked Ray.

Still, I didn't see how Ray could stand it. They didn't have any of the things Ray used to love, like cool shoes and guacamole and mocha lattes and television news. They didn't even have a TV. They didn't have many books either, and most of the ones they had had titles like *Inspirations for Christian Women* and *How to Bring Our Kids to God.* I hoped that last one wasn't Ray's, but it probably was, since every Sunday she still dragged me off to the Fellowship of the Redeemer and Mrs. Prescott's class. I tried citing the United Nations Convention on the Rights of the Child, but Ray said we hadn't ratified that treaty yet.

Ray was flourishing like the green bay tree. That's what she called it. It's from one of the Psalms. The bay tree spreads its roots everywhere and stays green even in winter. Mr. Peacock said that all that meant was that she was as happy as a pig in—at which point he pulled up short when Mrs. Peacock gave him a really awful look—and then he said in mud. Mud is what the Redeemers were, as far as Mr. Peacock was concerned. Mr. Peacock said that a real church was a building built proper for the purpose, with a steeple on it and a bell. He also said, when I was in the bathroom and wasn't supposed to hear, that a decent mother with an ounce of human feeling didn't run off and leave her little girl, and that if he had a daughter like me, he wouldn't sit around in a shed painting pictures that looked like something a bird did on a windowpane. He'd get off his rump and go to work.

It was while I was traveling back and forth between Boone and Ray that I became Subject #3 for Polly Pelletier.

The Casual Clip Shoppe on Main Street, that Polly's mother owns, is a meeting place for women, like Pierre's Barber Shop and Café three doors down is a meeting place for men. People drop in all the time while they're out shopping and have tea and coffee, because Polly's mother has a hot plate and a coffee machine, and they sit around on little wicker chairs and gossip and read the magazines. If you want to know anything about who's getting married or divorced, or who's having a baby, or what your most flattering colors are, or whether or not capri pants are still in, the place to go is the Casual Clip Shoppe. You can get diet advice there, like whether to try Atkins or South Beach or Jenny Craig, or find out how to cook eggplants or where to have a chair upholstered, or get a list of names of responsible teenagers who babysit. You can also get a haircut or a manicure or have your ears pierced. Polly also wanted her mother to learn to do tattoos, but her mother said over her dead body. So when Polly and Sara got their matching rosebuds, they had to go across town to Frank and Frank's Tattoos.

Frank and Frank are really Franklin and Frances Jane. They have a baby named Harley and two little dogs.

Polly and her friends hang out at the Casual Clip Shoppe all the time. Polly's mother lets them try out all the nail polishes and the facial masks and the hand creams, and Polly helps out by putting towels in the dryer and sweeping the floor. I never hung out there much, since I was never one of Polly's real best friends, but I always liked it when Ray took me there. Polly's mother would call me sweetie, and once she said I had classic cheekbones like Michelle Pfeiffer. I look about as much like Michelle Pfeiffer as Andrew looks like Brad Pitt, but it was still nice of her to say.

On Mondays the Shoppe was always closed, so that's when Polly had the run of it for her science-fair project, provided she cleaned up afterward and didn't put sludge down the sink. So we all met there after school, Sara Boudreau, who was Subject #1 and dressed just like Polly in black jeans and an Indian top with embroidery, Claire Thibodeau

(#2), me (#3), Angelique Soulier (#4), and Celeste Olavson (#5).

Polly had her project all planned on little sheets of paper, with who got what chemicals and for how long. We all sat in a row on chairs, wearing the Casual Clip smocks, which are bubblegum-colored, while Polly worked on our hair. It took an amazingly long time to do five permanent waves, and at one point Polly's mother came in to see how things were going and brought us pizza.

All the time that Polly was wrapping our hair up on different-colored plastic rods and making us sit around with plastic bags over our heads, we talked. Polly told us all about her future line of clothing, Polli with an *i*, and showed us the sketchbook she keeps in which she records her fashion ideas. One of her ideas was a puffy silver pantsuit that looked a lot like Andrew's last Halloween costume, the one that said, "Feed me, Seymour."

Then we talked about which famous person we would most like to have for a boyfriend, and I picked Gilbert Blythe from *Anne of Green Gables.* Then we all talked about our favorite books and our favorite movies and the qualities we thought were important in the person we might want to marry. Polly wanted someone with style and good taste in clothes, Angelique Soulier wanted someone who is fond of animals, and Celeste Olavson wanted a beefy athlete with no morals, though that's not exactly the way she put it.

I said I didn't think I'd ever get married, which made everybody get uncomfortable and change the subject. Because, as I said, everybody in town knows all about Ray and the Redeemers and Boone.

Then we talked about the world's big questions.

Claire Thibodeau, whose parents have peace-sign stickers plastered all over their pickup truck, said that the biggest question was, "How do we get people to live together in harmony?"

Claire is a pacifist and is not in favor of nuclear bombs.

To which Celeste Olavson's big question was, "Are you totally bats?"

Celeste, who is the descendant of Vikings and reactionary Republicans, is in favor of all the nuclear bombs we can get.

• • III • •

Then Angelique, who wasn't paying attention due to polishing her toenails silver with the Clip Shoppe nail polish, told a story about her grandmother running out in her underwear with a whiffle bat to chase a raccoon off her porch. So by the time we got back to the big questions, everybody had gone giggly.

Here are the rest of the Casual Clip Shoppe big questions:

> *Why is there algebra?*
>
> *Why is there braille at the drive-up ATM?*
>
> *Can vegetarians eat animal crackers?*
>
> *If God is everywhere, is he with you in the bathroom?*
>
> *If you throw a blue stone into the Red Sea, will it turn purple?*
>
> *How come in* Cinderella, *when everything changed back to pumpkins and mice and stuff at midnight, the glass slippers didn't?*
>
> *Why isn't a football shaped like a ball?*
>
> *How much wood could a woodchuck chuck if a woodchuck could chuck wood?*

Then the buzzer went off and we had to get back into the chairs to see what had happened to our hair. That was when, as Mr. Peacock would say, the mud hit the fan.

My hair, which is so straight you could pull pieces out and use them for a ruler, was curled up so tight all over my head that Polly couldn't even get a comb through. I looked like Ray's little faces with the porcupine quills, only curly. I looked exactly like a Brillo pad.

Sara's hair, which is naturally wavy, had turned into frizz. She looked like she'd been struck by lightning.

Celeste, who was frizzy to begin with, was now half frizzy and half straight, like one of those little kids' books where you can mix and match the pictures, and make faces that are half one thing and half another.

Claire, who has long limp blond hair, still had long limp blond hair, but part of it had turned orange.

Some of Angelique's hair came off with the plastic rods, so she looked as if she'd fallen under a lawn mower.

Polly looked at all of us and burst into tears.

Then everybody started yelling and crying and wailing, especially Angelique, who might have been going bald. Sara Boudreau picked up a pizza crust and threw it at herself in the mirror.

Then suddenly I started to laugh. I couldn't help myself. We all looked so funny with our awful weird hair and our bubblegum smocks, all stamping and moaning and wailing around like some mysterious tribal ritual out of *National Geographic* magazine. Then Sara started laughing, and Angelique and Celeste and Claire, and finally even Polly, so that pretty soon we were all roaring and holding our stomachs until Angelique said we had to stop or she would pee in her pants.

Polly took pictures of us all for her poster with her brother's digital camera. I thought that as science experiments went, it had been pretty much of a flop, but I figured she might get something for Most Inadvertently Hilarious Project and maybe the rest of us Good Sportspersonship Awards.

Polly's mother came in later to help Polly clean up and said that if we all came back tomorrow, she'd fix everybody up for free, and that Angelique shouldn't worry because a shorter hairstyle with layering would suit the shape of her face.

But I decided to leave mine the way it was. I've never cared that much what I look like, and besides I figured it might shake up Ray and the Redeemers.

Ray was starting to grow her hair long because there's a quote in the Bible about a woman's hair being her crowning glory. If Boone were a Redeemer, though, he'd have to cut off his ponytail. All the Redeemer men went around looking almost as scalped as Julie Laroche's love object, the essentially bald Jean-Claude Chevalier.

"Doth not even nature itself teach you, that, if a man have long hair, it is a shame unto him?" (I Corinthians 11:14)

But all the pictures of Jesus always show him with long hair.

Here is another big question:

> *If God is so all-knowing, why isn't he consistent?*

CHAPTER 13

> Honor thy father and thy mother: that thy days may
> be long upon the land which the Lord thy God giveth
> thee.
>
> — EXODUS 20:12

This was on the blackboard in Mrs. Prescott's room a couple of weeks later. In her Sunday school class, we'd been working through the Ten Commandments one by one. We'd already covered one through four — no other gods before me, no graven images, no taking the Lord's name in vain, and remembering the Sabbath day to keep it holy — and I was just waiting for number seven, because I was looking forward to watching Mrs. Prescott grapple with adultery. I'd noticed that the Redeemers were a little squeegy when it came to sex education.

The theme today was number five and obedience, which has never been a strong point of mine, having been raised by Boone and Ray, both of whom — at least until recently — were into encouraging kids to suspect propaganda, consider the issues objectively, and think for themselves. This got me into trouble back when it was time for me to fly up from Brownies to Girl Scouts, because of the Girl Scout Laws.

The Girl Scout Laws are to be honest and fair, friendly and helpful, considerate and caring, courageous and strong, and responsible for what you do and say, all of which I thought were fine. But then you have to promise to respect authority, which I thought wasn't fine at all. I mean, what if the authority is wrong? Like the Nazis or the Ku Klux Klan or even those advertisements on TV that are always telling little kids to eat those cereals that are made out of nothing but sugar and Red Dye No. 2.

I would probably still be stuck in Brownies if it hadn't been for Polly Pelletier's mother, who was the Girl Scout troop leader, and said I could skip that part as long as I promised to use resources wisely, make the world a better place, and be a sister to every other Girl Scout.

Boone was relieved, because he has a passion for Thin Mints.

"God tells us that we owe our parents unquestioning obedience because fathers and mothers know best," Mrs. Prescott said. "That's God's plan for the family. As the apostle Paul wrote in his Letter to the Colossians, 'Children, obey thy parents in all things.' Does anyone here have a story about a time when you obeyed your father and mother?"

I sat there looking at the clock. It had one of those minute hands that jumped with a click from minute to minute and I was practicing holding my breath between clicks.

"What about a time when you obeyed even though you didn't want to?" Mrs. Prescott encouraged. "But you did it because you knew that was God's commandment? Do you have a story, Marie?"

Marie said that last Friday she stayed home and babysat for her little brother.

"I really wanted to go over to my friend's house. But my parents were going out to dinner and they told me I had to stay home and babysit."

"How did you feel about that?" Mrs. Prescott said.

"Mad," Marie said.

"Obedience isn't easy," Mrs. Prescott said. "But you did the right thing. You did God's will and that brings great rewards. Does anyone else have a story to share? What about you, Octavia?"

I thought about how all I did just then was bounce back and forth like a tennis ball between Ray and Boone.

"What happens if your parents don't agree?" I said. "How do you know which one to obey?"

"Yeah," Wesley said. "My mom doesn't want me to ride on my cousin Ricky's snowmobile. But my dad says it's fine. My mom sure doesn't like it though."

Marjean shot me a look from under her braids,

and I waited to hear about a woman's place. Instead she bit her lip.

Then she said, "My dad wants Bud and Grover to go to college. But not me, even if I get straight As. A girl doesn't need college, he says. Not if she's going to be a good Christian wife and mother."

"Education is always valuable, Marjean," Mrs. Prescott said. "Perhaps if you spoke to Pastor Bruno . . ."

Pastor Bruno was the head of the Fellowship of the Redeemer. Ray liked him, but he reminded me of a rubber ball, the way he was always springing around and pumping his fist in the air.

"That's what my mother says," Marjean said. "She says what if someday I get left in the lurch like her sister Caroline, with four kids and no skills for anything but to be a maid in some rinky-dink motel. But my dad doesn't care. College costs money, he says. He doesn't even want me to have guitar lessons."

I looked at Marjean, who was breathing hard through her nose and glaring at her shoes. It occurred to me that maybe she wasn't as set on being Adam's Help Meet as she said she was.

"When I get out of high school, my father wants me to come work for him in the garage," Matt said. "But I don't want to work in the garage. I want to go to MIT."

"My mom won't let us buy a computer," Todd said. "She says all kids do with computers is look up porn sites and get themselves in trouble. How does she think I'm going to learn computer programming without a computer?"

I was going to ask if he had one at school. Then I remembered that Todd went to the Redeemer school.

"I think if God hadn't wanted us to have computers, he wouldn't have let us invent them," Todd said.

"Pastor Bruno has a computer," Ashley said. "He has it in his office."

"My parents wouldn't let me read the Harry Potter books," Kristin said. "But I read them anyway, at my friend's house. I didn't think there was anything wrong with them. I thought they were good books."

I waited for Marjean to say something about the glorification of Satan, but she didn't.

"He wouldn't have to pay for my guitar lessons," she said. "I was going to pay for them myself, with my babysitting money."

You could tell that Mrs. Prescott felt that things were beginning to get away from her. She had the look of a person who is out walking a very large dog when suddenly the dog sees a squirrel.

"We're talking about *obedience,* class," she said. "We're talking about how important it is to obey your parents even though you may not want to, because that's what God tells you to do. What about you, Ronnie? I'm sure you have a story about a time you obeyed your father and mother."

Ronnie was wearing another of his clip-on ties, this one with a pattern of motorcycles. In a few years, I thought maybe Frank and Frank of Frank and Frank's Tattoos might like one of those for Harley.

I sat there waiting for Ronnie to tell a story about how he'd minded his parents and God had rewarded him by giving him a five-dollar bill.

But Ronnie got quiet and red, and under his clip-on tie his Adam's apple started going up and down.

"Ronnie?" Mrs. Prescott said encouragingly.

Ronnie gulped as if he had a hard-boiled egg caught in his throat.

"My father hits my mother," he said, all in a rush. "Once he gave her a black eye."

Everybody looked at Ronnie.

Mrs. Prescott froze. You could tell she'd been expecting some story about taking out the garbage or feeding the dog.

"I don't think that's right," Ronnie said. "I don't think people should hit people like that, no matter who they are."

"No," Mrs. Prescott said faintly. "No, Ronnie, that's not right. That's something to pray about, Ronnie, and to see Pastor Bruno."

"He hit me too, when I tried to make him stop,"

Ronnie said. "But my mom yelled and told me to go in the bedroom with my little brother and shut the door."

There was a pause while everyone looked at Ronnie.

"Why don't we all say a prayer for Ronnie?" Mrs. Prescott said.

"I don't want a prayer," Ronnie said. "I just want to make him stop."

"God will do that if you have enough faith," Mrs. Prescott said.

I thought that was a lousy thing to say. After Ray having been a lawyer, I knew how to spot loopholes.

"What if his father doesn't stop?" I said. "Then will it be all Ronnie's fault because he didn't have enough faith? I think that's stupid. I think he should call the police."

"Yeah," Ronnie said.

"That's a big step, Ronnie," Mrs. Prescott said. "Pastor Bruno—"

"My sister Irene, before she got married, used to date this guy who punched holes in the walls when he got mad," Cathy Ann said. "He tried to punch Irene too. My dad didn't pray on it. He went out with a baseball bat and said to leave his girl alone and that bat was what he'd get if he ever showed his face at our house again."

"Did he ever?" somebody said. Maybe Marie.

"He sure didn't," Cathy Ann said. "We heard later that he got put in jail. And my dad told me when I'm sixteen if any boy ever gets mean like that with me, I'm to just let him know."

"Our session for today is almost over," Mrs. Prescott said. "Let's all join in saying a little prayer now, thanking God for our fathers and mothers and asking him to grant us the gift of obedience."

I poked Marjean in the arm.

"If you've already got the money, why don't you just take lessons anyway?" I whispered.

Marjean pursed up her lips and threw a furtive glance at Mrs. Prescott, who had her eyes closed. But she didn't say no.

I had a lot to think about. Like how maybe the Redeemer kids weren't so bad after all. Not like I'd thought they were.

"So what was class about today?" Ray asked.

"Obedience," I said. Which should have been the *O* word for the day.

But it wasn't.

Here were the words I picked instead: *Oppose, Outflank, Overturn,* and *Overcome.*

CHAPTER **14**

THE NEXT THING that happened was that Boone
and Ray made a lot of decisions for my own good
without consulting me. Boone didn't have the
heart to tell me about these decisions, so Ray did.
Having been a lawyer, Ray was more equipped for
confrontations.

I can't believe they thought I'd just quietly go
along with it all. I think maybe Ray was hoping that
some of the Redeemer indoctrination about obeying
parents had rubbed off. Mrs. Prescott must not have
told her what happened in the obedience class.

"Your father and I have had to make some decisions, Octavia," Ray said.

We were in the living room of the house Ray shared with Alda and Geraldine, sitting on the toad-colored couch that at night folded out to make the world's most uncomfortable bed. When you lay down on it, the mattress curled up around you so that it was like being a hot dog inside a very thin bun. I don't know what was under the mattress, but it felt like gravel.

"What decisions?" I said.

"About the future," Ray said. "About where and how we're all going to live."

"I like it where I am," I said. "I like Winton Falls."

"I know, honey," Ray said. "But it's not going to be possible for you to stay there. Finances are a lot tighter now that I'm no longer at the law office. Your father has found another house. It's smaller than our old house, but much more affordable, and there's space for him to have a studio. With some part-time work, he'll be able to handle it and still go on with his painting."

"I don't mind smaller," I said.

"It's a very small house," Ray said. "Your father thinks that you might be happier somewhere where you could have a little more personal space."

It was then that I realized that even though I didn't have an Ominous Knee, I had an Ominous Stomach. It wasn't twinging exactly, like Mr. Peacock's red-hot needles, but suddenly it felt as if it was full of electric eels. It had begun to dawn on me what this conversation was all about.

"Your father and I talked this all out, and we decided that it would be best if you moved in here with me for a while," Ray said.

I felt sick. Ray had sort of prettied it up, but I could see the bottom line. The bottom line was that Boone was willing to toss me to the Redeemers, just so he could go on painting his stupid masterpiece in his stupid shed. Or in some other smaller, more affordable shed.

"You think this will give me more personal space?" I said. "Living here in your living room on the daybed?"

"I've talked to Alda and Geraldine," Ray said.

"There's a little storeroom at the end of the hall that we're going to clear out for you. We'll move your bed into it, and your desk, and we'll put up some bookshelves for your books. There's a window that looks out on the yard. It's really very nice."

"What about school?" I said.

Because Ray's house is in Wolverton, which has its own schools.

"I can drive you to Winton Falls for a while," Ray said. "But eventually I thought you might like to try the Redeemer school. It's small, so you'd get a lot of individual attention, and you already know a lot of the kids who would be in your class."

"You want me to go to a school where they do science fair projects called 'Adam's Help Meet'?" I said.

I couldn't believe it.

Then I started thinking about the pod people. They were in a sci-fi story that Andrew told me about. It began with these spores that drifted down to earth from outer space. They would plant themselves secretly in your basement and then sprout and grow into pods that were perfect replicas of you. Then the pods would zap you and take your place. They looked like you and acted like you and talked like you, and nobody could tell that it wasn't you anymore, but really a pod person. Pretty soon the pods took over the world.

Maybe Ray was a pod.

"I'd like you to give it a try," Ray said. "I think it would be a good experience for you. I thought you were beginning to enjoy the Fellowship. Janet Prescott says you've been interacting well with the other students and sharing more in her class."

If Ray thought I was enjoying the Redeemers, she'd gone blind as a bat in a sack.

Or she was a pod.

"I don't want to move in with you and Alda and Geraldine," I said. "I think this is a terrible idea."

"I'm sorry you feel that way," Ray said, sounding hurt. "But it's really for the best, Octavia."

Boone's new house, the one that he had found without even telling me that he was looking for a new house, was just two streets away from our old house, which was now for sale. The new house had an apple tree in the yard and space for a garden, and there were three bedrooms, though one of them wasn't much bigger than a closet and it would have taken a NASA engineer to figure out how to fit a bed into it. Of the other two, Boone was going to sleep in one and use the other for a studio, since it had a hardwood floor and north light.

"That's nice," I said, sounding mean.

Boone was showing me over the place and pointing out how efficient the little kitchen was and explaining how eventually I could come to visit and stay in the closet, which by then he would have figured out how to turn into a bedroom. Probably by shrinking all the furniture dollhouse size, like in *Honey, I Shrunk the Kids*.

Eventually he noticed that I wasn't saying anything.

"What's the matter, Octavia?" Boone said. As if he didn't know.

"You figure it out," I said.

Boone sank down on the floor in the room that

was going to be the studio and leaned his head back against the wall.

"You know I love you, Octavia," he said. "It's just that I'm in a bad place right now."

Just for an instant, I thought about killing Boone. What kind of a bad place was *he* in, I thought. Here he was with a house of his own and a place to keep painting his masterpiece and an apple tree, while I was stuck in Wolverton with Alda and Geraldine.

I'd given up on my plan of running away to the bear diorama since Andrew had pointed out that the museum closed in winter and I'd probably freeze or starve to death in there. But I had other plans.

I could live at Andrew's house without anybody knowing, camping under his bed.

I could lie about my name, claim that I was an orphan, and eventually get adopted by a kindly couple on Prince Edward Island like in *Anne of Green Gables*. Somebody like Mr. and Mrs. Peacock, only Canadian.

I could win a scholarship to a boarding school somewhere far away, like London, and never come home again, not even for holidays, not even if the cruel schoolmistress made me sleep in the garret like Sara Crewe in *A Little Princess.*

"I'm so sorry, Octavia," Boone said.

He sounded miserable and confused.

But I didn't care.

"I hate you, Boone," I said.

I didn't feel like picking any *O* words that day. But if I had, they would have been *UnlOved, ThrOwn Over, AbandOned,* and *Outcast.*

CHAPTER 15

So there I was in Wolverton, living with three Redeemers and eight beans, which I watered every day and tried to treat fairly, except for the prayers. I kept track of their progress on a graph. Ray was proud of my interest in botany. She hadn't realized yet that the point of the experiment was to destroy her new life.

Life with Ray, Alda, and Geraldine was never much fun and sometimes it was just miserable. Part of the problem was that Alda and Geraldine, having been Redeemers a lot longer than Ray, had a lot more opinions about all the things I was always doing wrong. They didn't like my immodest clothes, which sometimes displayed unmentionable body parts like knees. They didn't like me arguing or asking questions because that was disrespectful. They were bothered that I still wouldn't make the Affirmation in Mrs. Prescott's Sunday school class because that showed that I was not in a state of grace. They wanted Ray to pull me out of the public school, which was a den of secular iniquity, humanism, and unsanctified peer pressure, and put me in the Redeemer school.

And they practically popped a gasket over the List. I wrote the List when I still believed in Andrew's theory about snapping and deprogramming, when I thought that maybe if Ray just heard enough logical arguments she'd give up the Redeemers. The List was my list of everything I could think of about religion that was bad. This is it:

Octavia Boone's List of Terrible Things Caused by Religion

1. *The Spanish Inquisition*

2. *The Crusades*

3. *Centuries of European religious wars*

4. *Witch hunts*

5. *Suicide bombers*

6. *Anti-abortion violence*

7. *Denial of rights to women, gays, and lesbians*

8. *Blocking the progress of science, like arresting Galileo and preventing stem-cell research*

9. *Attempts to deny atheists citizenship*

I stuck it on the refrigerator with the Cross of Faith magnets and left it for Ray, Alda, and Geraldine.

I figured that after that Alda and Geraldine would probably want to burn me at the stake, like Joan of Arc. I'd read her biography and part of her problem was immodest dress. She was caught wearing pants.

Instead they sent me to see Pastor Bruno.

* * *

Pastor Bruno had a wife named Barbara and six sons, though none of them was in Mrs. Prescott's class because they were all under ten. Pastor Bruno referred to them as his little Warriors of God, of which at least the little warriors part was right on, since they were all hellions, especially Michael and Gabriel, who were seven and twins.

Pastor Bruno was round and bouncy and enthusiastic and tan, and always reminded me of a cheerleader crossed with a basketball. Ray said he had a contagious energy, but I thought he must have been pretty exhausting to live with, the way he was always popping up and down all the time.

"Well, Octavia," he said. "I hear you're having a crisis of faith. That's what I'm here for, you know. To help people solve these problems. Would you like to talk about it?"

He was sitting behind his desk, which looked like the sort of desk Ray used to have in her law office, and I was across from him in a squishy leather chair.

"Not much," I said.

I was pretty sure that what Pastor Bruno thought was a problem and what I thought was a problem were two different things. Also I didn't think my problem was a crisis of faith. To have a crisis of faith, you have to have faith to begin with.

"It's easy to lose the way, Octavia," Pastor Bruno said. "You're not alone in having doubts. I've had them. We've all had them. I'm sure Mrs. Prescott has told you the story of Doubting Thomas, the apostle who refused to believe that Christ had really risen until he saw the holes in his hands. And our Lord said that the blessed are those who have not seen but still believe."

"I think Doubting Thomas was the only apostle with brains," I said. "I think believing without seeing is stupid. Scientists don't get to say, 'Hey, trust me, stuff is made out of atoms.' They have to have proof."

"But that's the nature of faith," Pastor Bruno said. "You have to let yourself go, Octavia. You have to open your heart. You have to give yourself over to Jesus."

So then I told him this story about Bertrand Russell. I'd heard it from Andrew, who, as I said, wanted to be a philosopher, and would like to be like Bertrand Russell. Though personally I don't think Andrew has a hope since Bertrand Russell was brilliant in math, and math is far from Andrew's best subject. It took him forever to learn his multiplication facts, and in geometry, he kept calling triangles little pointy things.

This is Andrew's Bertrand Russell story:

Bertrand Russell was an atheist. At his ninetieth birthday party, a lady who was sitting next to him leaned over and said, "So what if you're totally wrong? What if you die and you end up in heaven? What would you say to God?"

And Bertrand Russell said, "What I would say is 'Well, sir, you gave us insufficient evidence.'"

I hoped maybe Pastor Bruno would tell me that I was a hopeless cause. But he didn't. Instead he laughed so hard that I thought he would fall off his chair.

Then he said, "Octavia, I see you are going to be a challenge."

* * *

It was not long after that that Pastor Bruno decided to build Salvation Mountain.

Salvation Mountain started out as Deer Hill. As long as anybody could remember it had been called that, because there were always a lot of deer on it. People around here are not very imaginative when it comes to place names. Right here in town we have Park Street, that runs past the park; Church Street, that runs past the Congregational church; Pond Road, that runs past the pond; and Maple Street, that has a lot of maple trees. The pond is called Brown Pond because during the part of the year that there's no ice on it, the water is the color of strong tea. It always seemed to me that people should have been able to come up with something a little more creative. I said this to Mr. and Mrs. Peacock, and Mr. Peacock said then why didn't I go to town meeting and put my two cents in, which in his opinion would be a real relief from having to listen to everybody fighting over Alden Baines, who keeps putting logs across the road in front of his house and calling them speed bumps.

Andrew's idea was that Salvation Mountain

should be named Grand Teton. The Tetons are a mountain range in Wyoming, which is what Andrew was writing a report about in school, having picked Wyoming as his assignment out of Ms. Hodge's baseball cap. In French, *Grand Teton* means Big Tit. Andrew thought that was totally hilarious.

Deer Hill had been left to the Redeemers by a passed-on Redeemer named Maurice "Big Chip" Dupree. It had a bunch of dilapidated little cottages on it that Big Chip used to rent to deer hunters, and not much else except trees, weeds, and black flies. But Pastor Bruno had a vision. His vision was that all the cottages, where the deer hunters used to sit around with six-packs of beer, would be a Bible camp. There would be spiritual retreats for adults, uplifting activities for children, potluck suppers, and little benches set along a trail leading to the top of the hill, where people could sit and pray.

In my opinion, the *O* words for Pastor Bruno's vision were *Overly Optimistic.*

*   *   *

But once the snow melted, which it did early that year just to be ornery, Pastor Bruno had every able-bodied Redeemer out on Salvation Mountain on Saturdays, hauling brush and building benches and painting cabins. Ray and Alda and Geraldine all went, though Alda wasn't much help, due to shortness of breath and a low center of gravity that wasn't suited to hills.

Since they all went, I had to go too, unless it was one of the Saturdays I was staying with Boone.

CHAPTER 16

I DIDN'T LIKE living with the Redeemers, but at the time I didn't much like staying with Boone either. Boone didn't have a job exactly, but he was supporting himself by doing freelance financial work part-time. Also he was being frugal like Henry. He'd given up cable television and his subscription to *American Artist*, and he was heating with wood and eating a lot of rice.

When I asked him about this, but only to be polite, not because I cared, he said, "'A man is rich in proportion to the number of things which he can afford to let alone,'" which was a quote from guess who.

Boone still spent most of the rest of his time painting his masterpiece, though now in the bedroom upstairs instead of his shed. His whole house smelled like oil paint and turpentine. He always came down and cooked special meals when I was there, so I suppose he was trying. But we didn't talk much during them because Boone felt guilty and I felt mad.

It was nice to be in Winton Falls, though, because I could visit Mr. and Mrs. Peacock and see Andrew outside of school and ride my bicycle, which I couldn't do in Wolverton due to Ray's house being in a center of urban development with a heavy traffic pattern. People couldn't have pets there either, because of the cars, or if they did, they had to be indoors all the time or on leashes. Mrs. Peacock said that didn't sound healthy, breathing all those hydrocarbon fumes, and Mr. Peacock said to forgive him for saying so, but both my parents were acting like tomfools.

In May, on one of the Saturdays with Boone, we had our school science fair.

*   *   *

The Winton Falls Elementary and Middle School K–8 science fair, as I said before, is a big deal. There are announcements in the newspapers and on WCOW radio, and on the day of the fair there's a huge banner that says SCIENCE FAIR TODAY that hangs over the double glass doors at the school's front entrance. The banner is purple and orange, which are our school colors. I thought it looked nice, but Boone said those colors could only have been chosen by a color-blind philistine.

We spent most of Friday afternoon setting up, because the judges were arriving on Saturday morning at nine. There were three of them: Mr. Trahan, the geology teacher from the high school in Wolverton, who was freckled and bald and reminded me of a mushroom; Mr. Grumman, a retired engineer from IBM who had lots of fluffy white hair like Albert Einstein; and Dr. Cassidy, who looked a little bit like Hillary Clinton and was the president of a biotech company in Burlington.

The first thing you saw when you walked into the cafeteria, where all our exhibits were, was Aaron Pennebaker's radioactive spider, which was lime green and the size of a Frisbee. There was a big lime-green label pointing to the chelicerae, which are the parts spiders bite with, and Aaron's poster had before and after pictures of Peter Parker, showing him first as a normal person and then, after being radioactively bitten, as Spider-Man.

Aaron had also brought in his pet tarantula, Nicodemus, for purposes of comparison, but Nicodemus was so outraged by the science fair that he had crawled to the back of his cage and buried himself under his water dish.

Next came Polly Pelletier's "The Chemistry of the Permanent Wave" poster with all of our pictures looking like creatures from some hokey horror sci-fi show, like *Psycho Killer Amazon Women from Mars*. Our names weren't on them, just numbers, but of course, this being a small town, everybody knew who we were. Also my hair was still curly, though it had calmed down by now and didn't look quite so much like something you might use to scrub out a frying pan.

Then came a blank space where Jean-Claude Chevalier's poster of *CSI* corpses and blood splatters used to be, but that had been taken away because some of the teachers thought it was too gruesome for the little kids.

Then came Andrew's project, and I knew the minute I looked at it that it was going to be a disaster. The Wochaks, as I said, are prone to disaster, though usually this is not on purpose, but more like the time Andrew's mother forgot the garage door was closed and so backed the car right through it, or when Andrew's father cut down a rotten tree in the yard and it fell the wrong way and landed on the porch roof and smashed it flat.

Andrew's exhibit was called "The Anatomy of a Volcano: A Chemical Demonstration." His poster had diagrams of the insides of volcanoes, done in different-colored felt-tipped pens, and lots of pictures of famous volcanoes, printed off the Internet. In front of the poster was a cone-shaped papier-mâché volcano model the size of an armchair, with a hole in the top. Andrew must have used at least a ton of papier-mâché. A sign on the side read VESUVIUS, and there were a bunch of helpless-looking paper houses labeled POMPEII.

By the time I got there, all the judges were standing around it, along with the principal and Ms. Hodges and Andrew's parents and the members of the School Board, and Andrew had begun his demonstration.

"When I drop this mysterious substance into the mouth of my volcano, it will trigger a chemical reaction that imitates volcanic eruption," Andrew said.

I thought the word *imitates* was encouraging, because at least it showed that Andrew wasn't using real lava.

The mysterious substance was a lump of something about the size of a brick wrapped up in a paper towel.

"Is everybody ready?" Andrew said, and he gave a worried grin like he does before a disaster, like the time he set the dining-room curtains on fire with his magnifying glass. I think somehow, subliminally, Andrew always knows.

"Is everybody ready?" Andrew said again.

Everybody said they were.

Andrew waved the brick over his head.

"One!" Andrew said. "Two! Three!"

And he dropped the stuff into the top of the volcano.

For a minute nothing happened.

Then the volcano began to hiss and gurgle, like a pot coming to a boil. The three judges, who had had experience with science fairs before, hastily took several steps back, and so did Ms. Hodges and the principal and Andrew's parents, who had all had experience with Andrew. But the School Board, which should have known better, didn't move. So when the volcano erupted and belched out a huge fountain of red froth that drowned Pompeii and a lot of the table and the floor, it splashed all over Mr. Clover Harrison's brand-new fawn-colored spring suit.

That was pretty much the high point of the science fair.

Andrew explained later that it was just baking soda, vinegar, and red ink, but his parents still had to buy Mr. Clover Harrison a new suit.

Polly Pelletier won first prize in our division because the judges were impressed with her organization and understanding of disulfide bonds. Mr. Trahan, who, being a geology teacher, appreciates volcanoes, wanted to give Andrew an honorable mention for effort, ingenuity, and his description of pyroclastic flow, but Mr. Clover Harrison said absolutely not. Then he expelled Andrew from science fairs for the rest of his life, or at least until ninth grade, when he leaves this school district forever and goes to the high school in Wolverton.

Andrew's little sister Amanda won first prize in the grades 3–4 division for her vegetable solar system model, though luckily before two of Angelique Soulier's hamsters escaped and took a couple of bites out of Jupiter and ate the Earth.

Angelique's mother, when she saw her daughter's name on her poster as "Jennifer," called on all the saints, appealed to Angelique's father, and threatened to send Angelique to a French-speaking convent school in Montreal.

And Andrew wasn't the only one at the science fair who had a disaster.

My beans, as it turned out, didn't prove a thing.

CHAPTER 17

EFFECT OF PRAYER ON THE GROWTH OF
PHASEOLUS VULGARIS, THE COMMON BEAN

A Science Fair Project by Octavia O. Boone
Grade 7

So here's what happened with my beans.

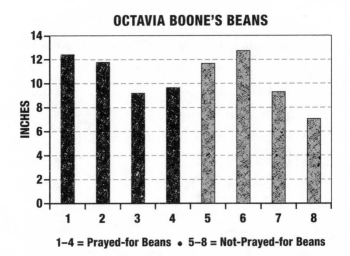

OCTAVIA BOONE'S BEANS

1–4 = Prayed-for Beans • 5–8 = Not-Prayed-for Beans

Of my four tallest beans, two of them had been prayed for and two of them hadn't. Bean #8, the shortest bean, hadn't been prayed for, but I was pretty sure that it was the shortest because it was on the far end of the windowsill where it didn't get as much sun and sometimes I forgot to move it around.

In other words, it didn't look like my prayers had had any effect on the beans at all. But, as Dr. Cassidy pointed out, there was no way of telling if this was because prayers really didn't work or because I'd been praying the wrong kind of prayer or because I just didn't happen to be very good at praying.

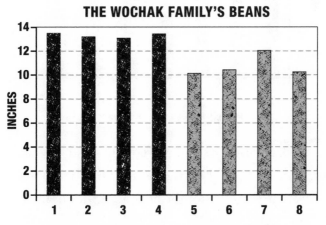

THE WOCHAK FAMILY'S BEANS

1–4 = **Meditated-for Beans** • 5–8 = **Not-Meditated-for Beans**

Of Andrew's parents' beans, the meditated-for beans, which you could tell because of the red feng shui ribbons around the pots, were all taller than the not-meditated-for beans. You would think that this was because Buddhism and feng shui were good for beans, but it turned out that Andrew's father, as well as meditating for the beans, had fed them Miracle-Gro.

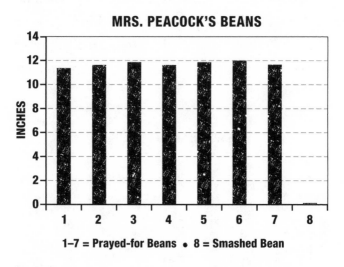

MRS. PEACOCK'S BEANS

1–7 = Prayed-for Beans • 8 = Smashed Bean

Mrs. Peacock's beans were all about the same size because she said that after the first couple of days, she felt sorry for the not-prayed-for beans and so she prayed for all of them. By then she only had seven beans, because Mr. Peacock had knocked one on the floor and smashed it while chasing a mouse with a broom.

Dr. Cassidy said that even though my results were not conclusive, it's always rewarding to see kids tackling big questions, and also she liked my graphs. I got an honorable mention.

I couldn't remember when I'd felt so miserable.

I guess I hadn't realized how much I'd been counting on those beans. I'd been so sure that I would be able to prove that prayer doesn't work and that, therefore, there is no God. Then Ray would see the light, drop the Redeemers, and come home. But I hadn't proven anything.

Some questions are beyond the scope of science, Dr. Cassidy said.

Then she asked me if I knew where the word *prayer* comes from, and when I said no, she said it was from the Old French word *preiere*, which means an entreaty of uncertain outcome. It's from the same place that we get the word *precarious*, which means something iffy.

In other words, you can pray until you're blue in the face, but God doesn't necessarily have to answer you.

In other words, it was a stupid experiment and I'd been an idiot.

After the science fair was over, I didn't say good-bye to anybody or wait for Boone. I didn't want to be around people. So I just left. I got my jacket and went out through the back door of the school, and across the empty playground, and then I walked. I walked for what felt like hours. I felt so awful that I didn't care where I was going, but I was too miserable to stay still. I slouched along with my head down, putting one foot in front of the other, and I'm probably lucky I didn't kill myself walking in front of a pickup truck or bumping into a tree.

When I finally looked up, I was in front of our old house. I guess I was so used to going there that my feet just did the thinking for me. The house was sold now, but the new people hadn't moved into it yet. The windows were blank and empty.

I walked around to the backyard. The purple lilac bush that Boone and I had planted for Ray one

Mother's Day was in bloom beside the back porch, and that made me feel even worse. I thought that things shouldn't be blooming like that, all lonely and by themselves, with nobody around to say how beautiful they looked and how good they smelled.

"You look great," I said to the lilac bush. "You smell wonderful."

I knew it was stupid talking to a bush, but I didn't care.

I walked across the grass to Boone's shed. The door was unlocked, so I pulled it open and went in. Everything was gone: Boone's easel and canvases and paint box and the jars he kept his palette knives and brushes in, and the corkboard where he used to pin up the pictures I'd done in school and postcards that friends sent him and photos of me and Ray. I sat down in a corner on the floor. The place still smelled a little bit like turpentine.

Then I saw a scrap of paper sticking up between two of the floorboards and I got the edge of it between my fingers and wiggled at it until I managed to pull it out. It was a photo, all creased and bent, that must have fallen off the corkboard. It was of Ray and Boone and me on a picnic. Boone had a deviled egg in one hand, and his other arm was around me and Ray. Ray was wearing jeans and a T-shirt and she was squinting because the sun was in her eyes and she was laughing. We were all laughing.

Suddenly I couldn't stand it anymore.

I hated having feelings. I wanted to be like Data in *Star Trek*, who was an android and never had any emotions at all.

But it was too late.

Right then I had so many feelings that it was as if they were all too big for my skin. It even hurt to breathe.

I dropped the photo on the floor and I put my face down on my knees and I cried and cried and cried. I howled. I cried until I couldn't cry anymore and could only make little wheezy sounds like a broken accordion. I cried until it seemed I'd cried a whole ocean of tears, like Alice did in *Alice in Wonderland*. If I'd suddenly been shrunk down small like Alice was, I probably would have drowned. Then I was worn out, so I curled up on the floor of Boone's shed and put my head down on my arms and breathed in the dust-and-turpentine smell, which somehow felt comforting, and finally I fell asleep.

I woke up when the shed door opened, and when I looked up, it was Boone.

He walked over and sat down next to me, cross-legged on the floor. He took my purple-and-orange honorable mention ribbon out of his pocket.

"You forgot this," Boone said.

"What are you doing here?" I said.

"Looking for you," said Boone.

"How did you know where I was?" I said.

Boone said, "Lucky guess."

Then his eyes slid past me and he reached out and picked up the photo that I'd dropped on the floor when I started to cry. He looked at it for a long minute and then put it down again.

"So tell me what's going on with you," Boone said.

So I did. It just poured out of me, like Niagara Falls.

"You abandoned me," I said. "You and Ray. Both

of you. You just went off to do your own things and you never cared about me. You never cared what I thought. I hate living in Wolverton. I hate being with Alda and Geraldine. I hate the Redeemers. I don't want to go to the Redeemer school, where they teach how the Grand Canyon was made by Noah's flood and how there were people around with the dinosaurs. I don't want to think like that. I don't believe that people go to hell if they dress up on Halloween and I don't believe women are supposed to stay home and serve men. I don't believe in being obedient all the time and never asking questions and I don't think it's a sin if men have a ponytail."

I was beginning to cry all over again, which I wouldn't have believed possible.

I could feel Boone petting my hair.

"And the beans didn't work," I said. Wheezed.

"What's this about the beans?" Boone said.

So I told him the reason for the beans, how I thought if I could prove—really *prove*—to Ray that prayers didn't work and there was no God, that she'd give up the Redeemers and change back to the way she was and come home and we could all be the way we were.

"Oh, Octavia," Boone said.

He reached down and pulled me sort of partway onto his lap, where I didn't fit anymore because I'd gotten too tall.

"I'm too big to sit in your lap," I said. Snuffling.

"You're just right," Boone said.

He petted my hair again.

"Listen," Boone said. "I've been offered a job with a financial firm outside of Burlington. It's full-time, with a good salary and benefits. I'd be working in an office, though, so I wouldn't be around every day when you got home from school. But you could go stay with the Peacocks in the afternoons if you didn't want to be on your own."

"You mean I can live with you?" I said.

"I'm sorry," Boone said. "I never meant for this to happen. I've been crap-all at being a dad. I guess I've just been hoping that she'd come home too. But she's not. She's made that pretty clear."

"What about your masterpiece?" I said.

Boone tightened his arms around me, and when he spoke, his voice was sort of choked, but that might have been because he was talking into my hair.

"You're my masterpiece," Boone said.

CHAPTER **18**

I WISH I COULD SAY it was all as easy as that, but it wasn't.

The first problem was that Ray didn't agree about me living with Boone.

"I'm sorry, Octavia. I don't think that's a good idea," she said. Which meant no, and she wouldn't budge off it, because Ray will never admit she's wrong. When she gets that way, she's like a stone wall.

The second problem was Alda and Geraldine, who backed her up, talking all the time about custody and responsibility and what it meant to be a good parent and the moral character of artists. Alda and Geraldine were not big on artists. They said artists were always abandoning wives and children and having mistresses, like Paul Gauguin, who dumped a wife and five kids to go paint in Tahiti, and Picasso, who was a terrible family man. Also artists were always painting naked pictures that might just as well be straight out of *Playboy* magazine and unholy pictures that were even worse than that but they wouldn't say how in front of me.

"Boone doesn't do that," I said.

Because in the first place if anybody abandoned anybody, it was Ray, not Boone. Also even if Boone's paintings are of naked women, you can't really tell.

But it wasn't just the paintings.

There was also the welfare of my soul, which according to Alda and Geraldine was in peril, since those who chase after false gods and idols will burn in hell. Boone was chasing after false gods. So were Andrew and Andrew's parents and Aaron Pennebaker and his family, because they're Jewish, and everybody in Winton Falls who's Roman Catholic, and

Dr. Cassidy, who does stem-cell research and wears pants, and all the Muslims and Hindus and Buddhists and everybody else in the world who wasn't a Redeemer.

I didn't think that was giving God much credit.

I mean, if there is a God and he really is the maker of the entire universe, wouldn't you think he'd be smart enough to give people the benefit of the doubt? Maybe you get to heaven and he pats you on the back and laughs and says, "Well, you did your best, but all that burnt-offering stuff was kind of silly," or, "Good try, but I'm actually not at all fussy about hair."

The real problem, though, was not Alda or Geraldine. It was Dr. Bethany Gilcrest of the Educational Center for Biblical Parenting.

Dr. Gilcrest was a Christian psychologist whose specialty was the Willfully Defiant Child. She ran a counseling service for parents who had them, which luckily for me was located in Fort Lauderdale, Florida, which is sixteen hundred miles from here. She also wrote a lot of articles about them, all with her picture on the front page. She had fluffy platinum-blond hair and false eyelashes, of which Mr. Peacock said a woman who puts those on her face is no better than she ought to be.

Geraldine brought home all the copies of *Biblical Parenting Magazine* with Dr. Gilcrest's articles in them from her office for Ray. On the cover of one issue was a smiling mother wearing one of those pinafore aprons with ruffles over the shoulders, and a little kid with her fists clenched and her face all scrunched up and she was stamping her feet. Over the mother's head was a thought bubble with a picture of Jesus in a field of flowers. There wasn't a thought bubble over the kid's head, but if there had been it would probably have had something like an exploding nuclear bomb. "See article, page 8," it said.

So I turned to page eight and began to read.

"In a battle of wills between parent and child," wrote Dr. Gilcrest, "it is imperative that the parent win. The defiant child is displaying a lust for power and independence that has no place in the home. He must be made to understand who is in charge and compelled to behave in an appropriately respectful manner."

I thought Dr. Gilcrest sounded more like a prison guard than a parent. I wondered if she had any children. If she did, I hoped they were lusting for power and independence behind her back. I hoped they were stockpiling graham crackers and digging a secret escape tunnel in the backyard.

"Do not lose your confidence," Dr. Gilcrest went on. "The Lord gave you this difficult child in order for you to mold him into a faithful servant of Christ. Your task will not be easy, but know that with the Lord's help, you will prevail."

I figured that the more Ray read that stuff, the more I was doomed.

This went on all through the last weeks of school. By then it was June and the days were getting warm. Boone planted a garden in his new tiny yard, with tomatoes and peppers and a lot of lettuce, and a pumpkin vine along the fence so that we could have our own pumpkins for Halloween. Though I figured the way things were going, I'd probably be spending Halloween in Pastor Bruno's House of Sin.

Ms. Hodges started reviewing everything we'd

learned all year, so that we wouldn't blacken her name in front of Kate Choquette and Roger Richardson, who team-taught eighth grade. But I had a hard time concentrating, thinking how next year I might not even be around. By then I might be going to the Redeemer school and learning creationism and writing essays about Adam's Help Meet and wearing *Little House on the Prairie* dresses like Marjean's.

I don't mean that I didn't like *Little House on the Prairie*. It's just not my fashion style.

Andrew tried to help by coming up with a really lousy plan for smuggling me out of town that involved a false moustache, a rope made out of bedsheets, and the Greyhound bus station.

But before he managed to talk me into trying it, which I was considering, we had the fight.

Not me and Andrew.

Me and Ray and Alda and Geraldine.

It happened at dinner, which was lentil soup, which I hate because it looks like toxic sludge, and I was picking at my food. Which is hard to do with lentil soup, because it's all just sitting there in a bowl and there's nothing you can hide under anything. I was taking teeny little spoonfuls and hoping nobody would notice.

I must have been drooping over my soup bowl looking miserable, because Geraldine asked me to please sit up and stop looking so glum.

"Octavia," she said. "You've been a wet blanket around here for weeks. Do you realize how hard this is for all of us?"

"I just don't like lentil soup," I said.

"I think it's more than that," Geraldine said.

"Gerry, I've got this under control," Ray said.

"I don't think you do," Geraldine said. Then she turned to me. "Do you know how hard it is for us to see what your mother is going through?"

"Like what?" I said. "What is *she* going through?"

I thought Ray was pretty much getting exactly what she wanted.

"She wants nothing but what's best for you," Alda said. "She loves you. She's been nothing but patient and understanding. It hurts her to see you so angry and uncooperative and resentful."

"Separations are hard on kids," Ray said. "It's a difficult transition."

"It's not a transition at all unless there's some effort on Octavia's part," Geraldine said.

"We all know this isn't easy for you, Octavia," Ray said. "We're just trying to help."

It didn't feel like help to me. It felt like ganging up.

"Help how?" I said. "You always said people should make up their own minds about things."

I could hear my voice getting stupid and wobbly.

"I don't see what you see," I said to Ray. "I'm not a Redeemer. I don't want to be a Redeemer. I don't want to be here."

Nobody said anything. They all just looked at me.

"Ray, I want to go home," I said.

I put my forehead down on the table next to my bowl of lentil soup because I didn't want to look at anybody anymore.

I heard them all talking over me, and Geraldine telling Ray to be firm and quoting from Dr. Bethany Gilcrest. I shoved back my chair, got up from the table, and ran upstairs to Alda and Geraldine's storeroom, which I wouldn't call my room because it never felt like mine. The little clay pots my beans used to be in were lined up on the windowsill. I'd stopped praying for them after the science fair, and Boone had planted them all in his tiny garden. Because of Henry, Boone has a soft spot for beans. But just then I didn't care.

I swept all the pots onto the floor and watched them smash. Then I threw myself down on the bed and lay there with my face in the pillow.

Downstairs they were all still talking, but I couldn't hear what they were saying anymore. It was just a babble of voices, with sometimes just a word or two coming clear. Gray steely-colored words.

Then there were quick footsteps in the hall, with Ray's heels like castanets, which always meant we were late for something important. They paused outside my door. The door opened, and Ray said, "Octavia?"

I kept my face in my pillow.

"Octavia," Ray said again.

She crossed the floor in two steps and sat down

on the edge of my bed and put an arm around me. I could smell her lily-of-the-valley perfume, which she's always worn ever since I can remember.

"You can go," Ray said.

At first I wasn't sure I'd heard her.

I picked my head up off the pillow.

"What?" I said.

"It's okay," Ray said. "You can go."

"I can go?" I said. "I can live with Boone?"

"You can live with Boone," Ray said.

I couldn't believe it.

"Why?" I said. "I don't get it."

Ray shook her head and gave me a funny, crooked little smile, but there were tears in her eyes.

And then she quoted, just like Boone always does.

She said, "Nothing is at last sacred but the integrity of your own mind."

CHAPTER 19

ON THE LAST SUNDAY IN JUNE, the Redeemers got together to dedicate Salvation Mountain, which had gone up faster than anybody ever dreamed. All the little shacks that used to be hunting camps were mauve and green cabins now, with built-in bunks, and there was a dining hall that could be used for lectures and church services and conferences, and a Spiritual Trail leading to the top of the hill.

Ray took me to the dedication. She was wearing an Indian print skirt with a ruffle and her hair had grown out some, but not enough yet to put into braids. She had it tucked behind her ears.

In a weird kind of way, it was fun. All my class was there: Marjean and Ronnie and Cathy Ann and Todd and all the rest. It would be wrong to say that they'd all had changes of heart after our obedience class and were thinking of not being Redeemers anymore, because they weren't and that wasn't what happened. But some things had changed.

Marjean's father had come around on the guitar lessons, after some backup from her mother and with the help of a quotation from the Psalms. ("I will sing a new song unto thee, O God: upon a psaltery and an instrument of ten strings will I sing praises unto thee" Psalms 144:9.) And Todd's parents had agreed to get a computer. Todd had had a more uphill battle than Marjean because there aren't any supportive Bible quotations about computers, but he managed to convince his parents that since computers were around at all, they must be a part of God's creation, and if God had created them, he obviously expected us to use them. He also promised that he wouldn't use it to gaze at immodest women but would apply it solely to godly purposes. He also pointed out that Pastor Bruno had one.

Other than that, though, everything was still pretty much the same.

At the end of the day I went off to climb the Spiritual Trail.

No matter by what name you call Salvation Mountain, it's really a beautiful hill. It's covered with maples and paper birches and little clearings with wildflowers, and at the top there's a flattish part where you can see the whole sky. When I got up there, there was Pastor Bruno in his JESUS SAVES sweatshirt sitting on a mauve-painted bench.

"Hi," Pastor Bruno said.

I didn't blame him for being up there, what with his six sons, including the twins Michael and Gabriel, rampaging around below. Though it seemed unfair to Barbara, his wife, no matter how willing she was to serve. I mean, it takes two.

"Hi," I said.

"I hear you're leaving us," Pastor Bruno said.

"Yeah," I said.

Pastor Bruno patted the seat beside him, offering me a place to sit down. The stars were beginning to come out. I could just see the Big Dipper.

"So is this all because of the List?" Pastor Bruno said. "What was it you called that again?"

I bet that Alda and Geraldine had been bending his ear.

"Octavia Boone's List of Terrible Things Caused by Religion," I said.

Pastor Bruno pursed up his lips and shook his head.

"But none of that is God, Octavia," Pastor Bruno said. "God didn't create evil. People did. God gave us free will, and sometimes people make bad choices. They use free will in the wrong way. People aren't perfect, Octavia."

"So what about those bad choices?" I said. "What do you do about them?"

"We pray," Pastor Bruno said. "And when God wills, our prayers our answered."

It didn't seem to me that prayers were going to do Ronnie much good. I said so.

"And sometimes," Pastor Bruno said, "God

answers our prayers by having a pastor take some-body's father aside and give him a good sharp talking-to."

"I don't think I believe in God," I said.

Pastor Bruno waved his hands around in the air.

"Then where did all this come from, Octavia?" he said.

"From the Big Bang," I said. "And then after billions of years, from evolution."

Pastor Bruno looked up at the stars. There were more of them now. I realized I'd forgotten to make a wish, and now I couldn't remember which star I'd seen first.

"'In the beginning God created the heaven and the earth,'" Pastor Bruno said. "'And the earth was without form, and void; and darkness was upon the face of the deep. And the Spirit of God moved upon the face of the waters. And God said, Let there be light: and there was light.'

"That's where the universe came from, Octavia. Everywhere I look I see the hand of God. How is it possible not to believe?"

An early mosquito whined in my ear. If there

was a God, I thought, I wished he'd seen fit not to use his hand to make mosquitoes.

"There's another Bertrand Russell story," I said. "It's about the Celestial Teapot."

"What's that?" Pastor Bruno said.

Andrew had told me about it. It came from an article Bertrand Russell wrote about religion. It was called "Is There a God?"

This is what Bertrand Russell said about the Celestial Teapot.

What if somebody claimed that somewhere out between the Earth and Mars there was a china teapot orbiting the sun? Nobody could see the teapot because it was too little to be seen even by the world's most powerful telescopes. So nobody could prove it wasn't there.

And then what if ancient books said that the teapot existed and people had to hear about it every Sunday and kids had to learn about it in school? Then pretty soon anybody who didn't believe in the teapot would be in trouble. People would think they were crazy or would say that they were going to hell.

I liked the story about the teapot. I had a picture

in my mind of the teapot out there in space, orbiting around and around. In my mind, it looked like the gingerbread-cottage teapot in Mrs. Peacock's teapot collection.

Pastor Bruno didn't say anything for a while. Then he sighed and patted me on the shoulder.

"I'll be praying for you, Octavia," he said. "I'll be praying that someday you'll find your way back to us. You'll be missed. And you'll always be welcome."

He got up from the bench.

"It's getting chilly," he said, "and they'll be lighting the bonfire down below. What do you say we get back to the others?"

"I think I'll stay here a little longer," I said.

I didn't think Pastor Bruno was right about a lot of stuff, but it struck me that he wasn't a bad person at all. I liked what he'd done for Ronnie and Ronnie's mother. I bet he'd been like Cathy Ann's father with the mean boyfriend, but without the baseball bat.

Suddenly I was glad that his name, *BrunO,* was an *O* word.

After Pastor Bruno left, I lay down on the bench and looked straight up at the stars.

I thought about my big questions.

Is there a God?

If there is a God, then why do bad things happen to good people?

If there is a God, which religion is the right religion?

Do people have souls or just brains?

What happens to us after we die?

Is there a purpose to life?

With all the thinking I'd done that year, I hadn't managed to answer a single one. Andrew says that's how you know your questions really are big questions. Still, it was disappointing.

All I'd figured out so far was that there was a lot I didn't understand. Just like Henry David Thoreau.

Like Henry said, "The universe is wider than our views of it."

That's what I believe.

CHAPTER 20

SO NOW I'M LIVING WITH BOONE. My bedroom isn't in the closet after all. Instead Boone squeezed his bed in there and put his bureau with all his clothes in it in the studio, since nothing else would fit in the closet once he squeezed in the bed. Since he has the studio, he said, it wasn't fair for him to have a big bedroom too.

He still spends time on weekends painting his masterpiece, so he hasn't lost hold of his dreams and aspirations like Henry was so worried about.

I don't go to the Redeemers anymore, though sometimes I get postcards from Pastor Bruno, and

Marjean sent me a tape of her playing guitar in a concert of Christian country-music songs. I thought it sounded pretty good, if you like that sort of thing.

I worried for a while about what everybody would say about us after all of this going on, since, like I said, this is a small town and everybody knows everything about everybody else. But Andrew said not to bother, because pretty soon somebody else's parents would do something crazy and everybody would forget about me and Ray and Boone, and Mr. Peacock, who spends two afternoons a week hanging out at Pierre's Barbershop and Café, said that whatever they were saying about us, it wasn't a patch on what they said about Mabel Butterfield when she started taking those belly-dance lessons at the Grange.

I don't see Ray very often just now because she's spending a lot of time traveling. She says it's important to spread the Word. Henry says "Do what you love" and I guess Ray is. I remember how Boone said "What is a good life?" is the world's most important question, and when I asked what the answer was, he said it was something you had to work out for yourself. I guess I'm glad Ray found her answer. But

I can't help wishing she'd found something else. Something maybe Boone and I could have shared.

I miss Ray. I miss the way we were before, with Ray heading out every day with her briefcase to her office at Banger & Moss, and Boone in his shed, painting, and me with nothing much to worry about other than my weird name.

"I wish things didn't have to change," I said to Mrs. Peacock.

Mrs. Peacock put down her dishcloth and wiped her hands.

"I used to feel just the same," she said. "It's no Sunday picnic, changing."

"Yeah," I said.

"I remember when I was your age, or a little older," Mrs. Peacock said. "My mama and daddy arranged for me to stay with the Tuttles up in town so I could go to the high school. There weren't any school buses back then, like they have now, and farm kids like me had to board in town if they wanted to get to school regular in the winter."

"Did you mind?" I said.

"Mind?" Mrs. Peacock said. "I was mad as

fire. They'd done all that behind my back, without so much as a by-your-leave. I didn't want to go. I fussed and I fumed and I dickered and I said I was fine just where I was and I didn't want to change. But my mama and daddy wanted me to have a good education.

"My mama said, 'Clara Jane, new things isn't easy and everybody gets a little bit scared. But if there wasn't any change, there wouldn't be any butterflies.'"

She filled the teakettle with water at the sink, put it on the stove, and turned the burner on under it.

"Neither of my folks got past fourth grade, you see, and I guess my mama didn't want me to spend my life as a caterpillar if I didn't have to."

I wasn't sure if she meant I was a caterpillar or a butterfly. But I got the idea.

What you believe about life, the universe, and everything is a big question that nobody can answer for you. I think you just have to work it out for yourself and sometimes it takes your whole life.

I still wish I could just peek ahead, like reading the end of the book first, and find it all out. But

Mrs. Peacock says you have to take things as they come, and that's not such a bad thing. "All in good time," Mrs. Peacock says.

There's a lot of other stuff to think about too. Like Ms. Hodges said way back last September, it's important to think about things and make plans because then you have a better chance of getting where you want to go.

I guess the best *O* words ever are still the ones from *The Wonderful O*. *LOve* and *hOpe* and *freedOm* and *tOmOrrOw*.

But I've got some more of my own, thanks to Boone and Ray and Andrew and Mr. and Mrs. Peacock and Ms. Hodges and Dr. Cassidy and Pastor Bruno and maybe even all the kids in my Redeemer class.

This is what they are:

GrOwing up
LOOking fOrward
MOving On